LANCE OF MYSTERY HOLLOW

LANCE

OF MYSTERY HOLLOW

BY
H. R. LANGDALE

Illustrated by
WOODI ISHMAEL

WILDSIDE PRESS

To

HAZEL LOUISE AND DOUG

CHAPTERS

LANCE OF MYSTERY HOLLOW

Chapter I

"Isn't it lucky you happened along!"

LANCE really woke when he felt the warm sunshine on his face, although for some time he had been aware that his insides had that disagreeable feeling which only food would banish. He kicked off the horse blanket, welcome enough through the frosty night but unbearably heavy now, and rolled out of bed to his feet. Except for the pair of tall, cowhide boots beside his bunk he was dressed for the day.

Boots on, he foraged in a stone crock for a large, flat, yellow-meal journey-cake and went out into the bright morning. Allowing himself one huge bite of the cake, he plunged his head into the icy water overflowing from a wooden trough standing beside the cabin and fed through the hollowed half of a birch trunk by the spring on the hill above. A towel, not very dirty, hung on a peg on the cabin door, and with it Lance vigorously rubbed his face and arms and dripping hair.

Then, picking up what was left of the journey-cake, he sat down on the flat top of a maple stump to consider plans for the day.

Below, in the valley, mists were rising slowly above the river. Ahead, beyond the nearer hills, Shrewsbury Peak lifted clear-cut against the sky. All about him, on grass and leaves, was spread the dewy lace of cobwebs. He could see for himself it was going to be good September weather.

"I can go after a buck," he said aloud, between satisfying bites, "or I can take up exploring of the Hollow where I left off, or I can, yes, I suppose I can go to town for more yellow meal at the grist mill."

But when he had thrust his hand into the pocket of his homespun breeches and brought out a few copper coins he shook his head.

"No," he said ruefully, "no going to town until I get me something to swap."

He was about to return the coins to his pocket when he noticed the one he had picked up a few days ago on the far side of the Ridge. It was easy to tell from the others because he had had to scrub it so thoroughly to find out what it really was. It had turned out to be like any copper coin, with a rising sun and a plow and the words "Vermontensium Res Publica 1786" on one side and a big eye with thirteen stars and the words "Quarta decima stella" on the other.

Finding the piece of money where he had, rather than the money itself, had been the amazing thing.

He had gone hunting and, some distance beyond the Ridge, whose descent he had made earlier in the day, he had scrambled through a tangled windfall into a tiny clearing beside a brook. There, right at his feet, a few inches from the water and partly embedded in the mud, had lain the round weathered bit of copper metal which was now the brightest of the few coins in his pocket.

He remembered how, even as he stooped to pick it up, the thought had popped into his mind, If I knew how this coin came here, I'd be on my way to finding out the mystery of the Hollow.

The mystery of the Hollow! Would he ever learn what it was?

Would his curiosity ever be satisfied as to what lay behind the grim warnings of the Valley Mill dwellers when they learned his father was planning to build a cabin in the Hollow? "Don't be settlin' there, Mister. Folks been shunning that place o' late!"

But when his father had questioned them, they had shrugged their shoulders and given vague answers about strange doings and queer noises and a hunch-backed man seen climbing the Ridge at midnight.

His father laughed and had not changed the site of their home, but, before he died so suddenly of the lung fever, he and Lance had decided to explore the Hollow foot by foot. Lance marked out with bits of charcoal a huge map on deerskin of the record of their findings, and pegged it on the cabin wall. For the two of them, returning late one night from a day spent hunting, had seen, silhouetted against the moon-lighted sky, not one queer, stooped-over figure, but two.

With the last crumb of the journey-cake, Lance reached a decision. "I'll take old Eagle-eye and hike over the Ridge and pick me up something to swap for meal. Tomorrow I'll go to town, and the next day I'll piece out the Map some more."

Eagle-eye, his father's gun, stood in the corner behind Lance's bunk and, on his way to get it, Lance paused to look at the Map.

The hide on which it was drawn had been that of a twelve point buck and covered more than half of the cabin wall opposite the door. The Map itself was as yet little more than an irregular outline with a few crosses and circles and dots scattered mostly in the lower right hand corner as one faced it. These were variously labeled "Home," "Valley Mill," "Ox Road," "Chapelle's Gore," "Moose Pond," "Mill Creek Pond," "Squaw Hill," "Clarendon Gorge." Partly bisecting the entire map ran a wavy line marked "The Ridge."

Branching out from the area containing the cross labeled "Home," were several oddly shaped figures indicating sections of the Hollow already explored by Lance and his father, and a very few by Lance himself in the three months since his father's death. In one of the latter, the very last one, in fact, to be added, was a thin and crooked line about one inch long with the words, "Copper Coin Brook", running along beside it.

"And that," nodded Lance, "is where I'll start from next time. I'll follow the brook both up stream and down. That coin didn't fall out of the skies like a meteor."

With Eagle-eye on his shoulder and the last of the journey-cakes in his pocket, Lance set out, throwing one last reluctant glance toward the Ridge beyond which lay Copper Coin Brook and the vast tangle of wilderness that was the Hollow. After all, he reflected, a string of rabbits or squirrels would buy him enough meal from Miller Robins to make a fortnight's supply of cakes. Then he would be free to spend his days as he liked.

The clearing where Lance's father had built their cabin was actually close to the curve of the rim of the Hollow. The narrow, grassy road which Lance followed through the woods began to climb at once. and, except for a slight thank-ye-marm here and there, did not really descend again until it reached the fork just this side of Chapelle's Gore which was not really in the Hollow at all.

When he reached the fork, Lance paused for a moment, pondering which way to go.

He had it in mind to work toward Moose Pond which would mean turning to the right and so passing the Chapelle farm. But passing the Chapelle farm was the very last thing in the world he wanted to do.

Every single time I go near those Chapelles, he reflected, I get mixed up in something which interferes with my own plans.

There had been the rainy morning when he had figured the pickerel would be biting like all get-out in Moose Pond. Whether they were or not he never learned, having spent the whole day chasing a miserable parcel of Chapelle hogs that had broken out of their flimsy pen and taken to the wood lot just before he appeared.

There had been the blowy afternoon when he had noticed, without at all wanting to do so, that the hempen rope, filled too full with wet clothes, had pulled out its peg in the side of the lean-to and fallen to the ground. What a job that had entailed, with the twins, Jacques and Jean, shrieking, and their yellow dog, Boney, yelping like mad about his heels, and M'ma Chapelle waving her arms and shouting at him.

The last time had been the worst of all. Mathilde Chapelle, who was old enough to know better, had climbed to the top of a butternut tree, only to fall out of it with wild screams at his very feet. And the pity of it was she hadn't even broken anything.

No, it would be much more sensible to turn to the left, and confine his hunting to the area between Squaw Hill and Clarendon Gorge.

On the other hand, there was always the chance that, once safely by the Chapelle home acre, he would find Cherry tossing her proud little head above the pasture bars, half-ready to be coaxed by a bit of journey-cake into standing still long enough to have her nose stroked.

Lance drew a deep sigh. One of the things he had found hardest to do since his father died was to make his own decisions. Before that there had always been some-one to say, "Today we'll haul out the spruce stump," or "You'd better hitch up, son, and go to the grist mill afore we're plum out of meal."

He fished the bright copper coin out of his pocket. "If the plow lights on top, I'll go to Moose Pond, and I'll just pay no heed to those Chapelles. If it's the eye and the stars come up—"

But instead of tossing the coin into the air he put it sheepishly back into his pocket. "No bit of ornery ore out of the ground is going to make up my mind for me," he said aloud. "I'm taking the right hand road to Moose Pond."

It was very warm in the woods and Lance was glad when, after half a mile of following the road which was little more than a rutted trail, he came to the crest of the hill. There he could sit down on a huge slab of country rock and feel the wind in his face. Always his father had rested his horses here, and Lance could still see where they had cropped the lower branches of the young beeches.

Below him ran the thin silver thread of Mill Creek on which the grist mill stood. Nearer at hand curled a lazy plume of smoke from M'ma Chapelle's smoke house. It was but a step now to the small dwelling which P'pa

Chapelle had built several years ago and had left early last summer on some wild goose chase, according to his wife, from which he had not yet returned.

Again Lance was tempted to cut through the woods and circle back by way of Squaw Hill, and again the thought of little Cherry, satin-nosed, flyaway Cherry, with the white streak down her forehead, held him to his former decision.

Raising Eagle-eye to his shoulder, he started down the hill.

Not a soul was in sight as he came abreast of the squat, one-storied farmhouse set a few yards back from the road. Lance drew a deep sigh of relief and quickened his step. Once around the curve without being seen, he would not be known to have passed at all, and he could stop at the pasture bars as long as he wished. He felt in his pocket. Yes, the journey-cake was crumbling, but still there.

He was halfway around the curve when he saw there were figures in the pasture, and they were moving as if in a procession of some sort. The twins, Jean and Jacques, were there, and the dog, Boney, and Mathilde, and M'ma Chapelle who was carrying an old flintlock left at home by her husband. Cherry was nowhere to be seen.

Curiosity got the better of Lance's desire to escape notice. He stood stock still, staring at them with puzzled eyes. Were they squirrel or rabbit hunting like himself? That hardly seemed likely with plenty of meat at hand, what with geese and hens and jerked beef and pork, and now and then a young pig. Could a painter have come out of the woods during the night and carried off a calf or a sheep, and were they after him now? Having come once, he would come again; and there was always the bounty of $20 to be had for his skin.

The backs of all the Chapelles were toward him as they climbed the rocky slope in the direction of the woods. Suddenly, for no reason at all that Lance could see, Mathilde turned around, caught sight of him, and stopped short.

The next moment, with an ear-splitting shriek, she was flying toward him on the run, her two long black braids streaking out behind her.

"Lance! Oh, Lance!" she was screaming. "Ma's got to shoot Cherry! Now she won't haf to. You can do it. M'ma! M'ma! Lance is here and he's brought his own gun! Oh, Lance, isn't it lucky you happened along!"

Chapter II

"Iffen you know what is good for you—"

SHOOT CHERRY! Lance felt his knees go a little weak, and he made no movement to climb over the bars.

Mathilde stamped her foot impatiently. "Do hurry up, slowpoke! There's just no use letting the poor thing suffer any longer, even if she is a wild one. Ma's fairly sick over doing it her own self on account of fearing Pa's flintlock won't shoot straight. Besides, Pa cautioned her to take more care of Cherry than of anything else on the place, and Ma says we shouldn't have left her out to pasture nights, and—well, thank goodness, Lance, you've decided to come!"

For Lance was lifting his long legs over the fence rail. "Whatever happened, Tilda?" he asked soberly.

As they climbed the slope toward the little group who waited for them, Mathilde told him what there was to tell. "We don't really know whatever did happen, or when. Nobody came down to the pasture yesterday, but this morning we did, and Cherry was just nowhere to be seen. When we finally did find her, she was lying flat on the ground up in the Little Pasture on the very top of the hill, and—but you'll see for yourself, Lance."

Five minutes later, Lance did see. Cherry, her moist chestnut flanks rising and falling, was stretched on her side. One leg, held at an unnatural angle, was swollen to twice its usual size a short distance above her shapely little hoof.

Lance knelt down and placed his hand on the hot, injured limb, while Cherry rolled her brown eyes until the whites showed, and struggled violently to get to her feet.

"There's just nothing to do but to put her out of her misery," declared M'ma Chapelle. "She's never been much use. Won't let anybody gentle her and shams lame when she's haltered. The only thing is—" a troubled expression came into her eyes—"my husband sets great store by her. Called her 'Cherie', meaning 'dear' in French, and said she had the makin' of a fine mare. When he comes back, if so be he ever does come back—" she broke off without finishing to shrug her thin shoulders and glance vaguely in the direction P'pa Chapelle had taken so jauntily many months ago.

Lance rose to his feet. "I'd like to have a try at curing her, ma'am. Looks to me like she stumbled in a chuck hole or maybe over a rotten log. One of our horses was hurt like that, and Pa doctored it into being all right again. If her leg isn't broken, seems like it's worth a try."

Mathilde tossed her head. "Since when did you learn to be a doctor, Mr. Lance?"

But Mathilde's mother hesitated. "How'd we ever get her down to the lean-to?"

"On the stone boat, ma'am. Shall I fetch it up with

the oxen?" Lance scarcely waited for M'ma Chapelle's doubtful consent before he was off like an arrow down the hill.

The long shadows were falling across the clearing when Lance reached home that night. He brought no squirrels or rabbits with him. He hadn't fired a shot all day. He hadn't, in fact, gone hunting at all.

There had been, to begin with, the business of roping the frantic colt to the low sledge, and hauling her from the Little Pasture to the lean-to. Then there was the binding of the swollen leg with strips of unbleached cloth woven on M'ma Chapelle's loom and soaked in a solution of balsam of pine, Epsom salts, black cherry water, and powdered red chickweed.

Lance wasn't at all certain of the value of either the cherry water or the chickweed, but he did remember watching his father dissolve the salts and then mix the solution with the thick pungent balsam sirup.

However, "There's nothing like powdered red chickweed," M'ma Chapelle insisted, "stirred into seven parts distillation of black cherries." So these, too, had gone into the concoction.

"A few drops of skunk's oil would help," she added.

But Mathilde turned up her freckled nose. "The smell is already enough to kill her, Mr. Dr. Lance!" she declared pertly.

It had been a long struggle to bandage the swollen leg, with the colt fighting madly against something she couldn't understand and kicking crazily in all directions at once, her teeth bared and her eyes wide with pain and fear.

Afterwards Lance spent an hour coaxing her to drink water from an iron kettle, but without success. Cherry, used to the pasture brook, would have nothing to do with the kettle. Lance finally gave up the attempt, turned to take his gun and go.

M'ma Chapelle stopped him. "You'd better stay on for some fried salt pork 'n milk gravy, Lance." The twins draped themselves on each arm, and even Mathilde threw him a saucy smile that was as much of an invitation from her as he could expect. Besides, the very thought of "fried salt pork 'n milk gravy" after so many meals of nothing but journey cake made his mouth water.

So Lance stayed. "I'll spend the afternoon getting those squirrels and rabbits for Miller Robins," he promised himself.

But when he had eaten, M'ma Chapelle must ask his advice about how to store her potatoes so they wouldn't turn green and poisonous; must show him, with a worried expression on her thin face, how her supply of seasoned logs was dwindling and winter coming on; must explain, and this took the longest of all, how she didn't know anything about farming, being a city girl from Burlington where there were as many as five hundred persons and two churches, when she had married her husband Pierre. He was a Frenchman from Quebec and never had she dreamed he'd want to leave such a big city as Burlington to take up land in the wilderness and then wouldn't be satisfied but must go hunting a new homesite out West somewhere in New York state. Now here it was fall, and he wasn't back yet, and the twins were too young and 'Tilda too flighty to be any help; and there was always something happening like this accident to Cherry, who would likely never be good for much again—

"I guess," said Lance to himself when he was at last on his way back home, having decided to postpone his hunting until another day, "I guess she hasn't had a soul to talk to for quite a spell, except that 'Tilda who doesn't keep quiet long enough to listen to anybody. I'm glad, though, I live all of three miles away."

Then he remembered that he had promised to look in on Cherry the next morning, and drew a deep sigh. Those Chapelles didn't plain deserve a wonderful little horse like Cherry, leaving her so long out in the pasture all by herself. If Cherry belonged to him—but that was such a wonderful thought it took Lance's breath away.

He had hardly come out of the woods into the small clearing before he realized something was wrong. Or, if not wrong, at least queer and disturbing. He couldn't immediately detect what it was that made him think so. The cabin seemed just as he had left it, with the door and the one window both tightly closed. The water, flowing down from the spring on the hill, was splashing over the edge of the trough just as usual. The not very dirty towel—

But the towel was gone. Unable to believe his eyes, Lance stared at the empty wooden peg beside the door, but no amount of staring would hang the towel on the peg again. Had it blown down this windless day? He looked quickly around. There was no sign of it. Had some animal made off with it? Well, it would take a pretty tall bear, standing on his hind legs, to reach the peg. Besides, what would a bear want with a towel?

Then he noticed something else. The piggin from which he always drank had been dropped into the trough itself, instead of being laid athwart the cross pieces of the wooden support on which the trough rested.

There was no doubt about it. Someone, during his absence had visited the clearing, had taken a drink, and carried away the towel. Why had he come? Where had he come from? Where had he gone? Had he gone at all, or was he waiting at this very moment inside the cabin?

Suddenly Lance heard a sound behind him. A soft little sound, not at all threatening in itself, yet enough, under the circumstances, to make his heart pound like a hammer in a nail driving contest. Something was coming toward him out of the very woods where he had just been.

Lance swung around, lifting old Eagle-eye with one hand and reaching for his powder horn in his breeches pocket with the other. Then he let both arms fall to his sides.

"You!" he exclaimed in disgust, as the pint-size body of Boney, the Chapelles' yellow cur, bounced out of the underbrush.

For an instant Lance instinctively blamed the vanished

towel and the misplaced piggin on Boney. Then common sense reasserted itself, and he glanced fearfully toward the cabin. Just suppose some vagrant had the notion to wait for his return, waylay him, get his gun—

"He won't get old Eagle-eye!" murmured Lance stoutly. "You come along, too, Boney."

Stealthily he approached the cabin, the butt of his gun snug against his shoulder, amiable Boney trotting obediently at his heels. Lance kicked open the cabin door and stepped over the threshhold. Falling twilight made dim the cabin interior, yet only one glance was needed to show that it was empty.

Slowly Lance went outside again.

There was a chance, of course, that his visitor had been some stray huntsman from Valley Mill, although hunters as a rule sought the Moose Pond area rather than the Hollow. But a huntsman from Valley Mill would not have taken away the towel, any more than he would take away a grist or hunk of brined pork. A towel was "property".

Lance sat down on the maple stump to think, while Boney scurried around as if he were really busy about something.

Black shadows were already high on the distant mountains, and the valley between the clearing and the Ridge was dark. Always at night the Hollow took on an added mystery for Lance, because it had been at night he and his father, and the Valley Mill folk, too, had seen the strange, stooped figures against the sky.

One by one he called to mind the few neighbors he had this side of Valley Mill besides the Chapelles. There were, of course, no dwellers in the Hollow except himself, at least, so far as he knew. He needed hardly the fingers of one hand on which to count them. There was the Indian family on Squaw Hill; there were the Tarbell brothers on Ox Road, and Old Molly on Teardrop Lake. Those were all.

Old Molly was so crippled with rheumatics she could barely hobble out to feed her creatures, a cow, a pig, and a handful of chickens. The Tarbell brothers, Amos and Abe, were known as hermits and had never been seen outside their own clearing. As for Indian Pete, his stolid wife, and round-faced boys, whenever they came they stayed overnight, wrapping themselves in their blankets and lying down under the pines at the Clearing's edge. Lance was sure they would not have touched the towel nor have moved the piggin so much as an eighth of an inch from its rightful place.

Ready to dismiss the whole incident as inconsequential and likely never to be explained, Lance shrugged his shoulders and walked toward the rotting log where Boney was delicately pawing at a moving stream of red ants. Here the ground sloped toward the woods, furnishing a natural run-off for the water spilling from the trough. The long grass, unmown since his father's death, lay flattened, and the leaves drifting down from the nearby maple, were moist and black.

Suddenly Lance stopped short, his eyes nearly popping from his head.

There, at his very feet, plainly outlined in the damp earth, was the imprint of a man's boot. Quickly Lance looked for another, and found it, but this time the impression made by the toe, being on firmer ground, was missing. Although he continued to hunt until it was too dark to see, he could find no others. The two he had already discovered, however, told him something from their location and the direction in which they were pointed. The stranger had unmistakably come to the clearing from the depths of the Hollow.

Lance carefully shut his door when he returned to the cabin, and dropped into place the bar which held it closed against any pressure from outside. He was even glad of Boney's company, and fed him the last of the journey cake crumbs in the bottom of the earthenware jar.

It was Boney who waked him in the morning, scurrying from one end of the cabin to the other, chasing bits of yellow paper.

Lance, only half roused, lay on his side watching him, glad that the sunlight streaming through the window promised a good day. For the moment he had forgotten the events of yesterday. Then he saw a crumpled piece of yellow paper on the floor beside his bunk and leaned down to pick it up. Puzzled as to where it had come from, he smoothed it out. There was writing on it . . . badly formed, unevenly printed letters straggled across it.

"IFFEN YOU KNOW WHAT IS GOOD FOR YOU, MR. BUSYBODY, YOU—"

The rest of the message had been chewed to bits by Boney.

Recollection of the missing towel, the misplaced piggin, the footprints in the soft earth rushed to Lance's mind in a flood.

He lifted his eyes unseeingly to the deerskin map on the wall, unaware for the moment of anything but the menacing scrap of paper he held in his hand. Suddenly his vision cleared, and he saw that someone, helping himself to the bit of charcoal on the cabin ledge, had criss-crossed the map from corner to corner with broad black smudges.

Chapter III

"You wouldn't by any chance be Mr. Busybody?"

"ARE you angry, Lance? Why don't you talk? Do you mind so much going to town? It *is* dull riding behind these old slowpokes. I do wish Cherry hadn't broken her leg and would let me ride her and I could go galloping, galloping madly down the mountain side! I think you *are* angry!"

"I'm not angry, and Cherry didn't break her leg, and I don't expect she will ever let you ride her, and that's very fortunate, because if you did go galloping down this mountain side you'd break all her legs, and probably her neck, too. Anyone lucky enough to own a colt like Cherry—" Lance shrugged his shoulders and returned to his thoughts.

He and Mathilde sat high on the hard wooden seat of the ox cart. In front, Wash and Jeff, the pair of small red Devon oxen, plodded slowly down the long, steep grade, the backs of their necks pushed hard against the yoke. Heaped in the rear of the wagon were grists for the mill, a rush basket of eggs to be exchanged for a bolt of calico at the store, and a coffee mill with a broken handle to be repaired at the whitesmith's. In Lance's pocket was a letter from M'ma Chapelle to her husband, addressed to Uticy, New York.

"Not that 'twill likely ever reach him, but 'twas the place he told me to send word to if anything went wrong, and his not getting back before winter sets in will be *everything* goin' wrong. I trust you more'n 'Tilda not to fergit it, and don't give it to anybody but the stage-driver hisself."

The day was cool and crisp. Here and there along the road side stood a sugar maple already turned to gold and crimson. From the depths of the forest on either side, came the chattering of Canada jays and once the sweet, delicate bell of the hermit thrush. Overhead, white clouds scudded across the blue. The weather was well suited to any sort of enterprise.

Here I am, Lance was thinking bitterly, taking care of those Chapelles again, when I have business of my own to tend to. If it hadn't been for looking after Cherry and so giving 'Tilda's ma a chance to ask me to go to town, I'd have been on my way over the Ridge this very minute. I might even have reached Copper Coin Brook and be started on exploring a new piece of the Hollow. After what happened yesterday, that vagrant taking my towel, smudging my deerskin map, and writing me threats even if I don't know what they were, on account of that mangy cur Boney, the sooner I find out what it's all about, the better pleased I'll be. "For goodness' sake, 'Tilda," he exclaimed loud, "can't you sit still for a single minute? You bounce about like—like—"

"Like a tumbleweed, Lance?"

"Like two tumbleweeds!" retorted Lance crossly. "Besides, we're down the mountain now. Yonder's Valley Mill."

It seemed only a few minutes later, even with the slow gait of the oxen, that they were crossing the creek through the newly built covered bridge and had come to a stop in front of the grist mill, whose great round broad-flanged wooden wheel could be seen turning slowly in the stream. There was a clean, malty smell of grain about the place, and a soft film of golden dust powdered everything, even Miller Robins himself, who stood in the doorway, his hands spread on his hips.

Miller Robins had a voice as big as his body. "So everybody in seven counties comes to town on stage day!" he boomed. "Stone's been grindin' since sun-up. Dump your grists inside and wait your turn. Warrant we'll get to you by the middle of the afternoon. Drivin' for Chapelles now, be ye, Lance?"

Before Lance could reply, 'Tilda spoke up. "Just this

once he is, Miller Robins, unless my father doesn't return before snow flies."

"Hmm!" grunted the miller, with what seemed to Lance a queer expression in his eyes. "Pierre Chapelle always did have an itching foot. 'Spect him back, do ye?"

'Tilda stared at him. "Of course we expect him back," she said quickly. "Unless the Yorkers kill him."

The miller broke into a great roar of laughter which shook his very sides. "Iffen the Yorkers don't kill him! That's over and done with now, Miss. We stood up for our rights alongside Ethan Allen and all is peaceable. Not," he added slyly, "that I'd trust them Yorkers too far myself!"

Lance, after unloading the grist, drove the wagon to the rear of the mill and left the oxen standing in the shade of the maples with a dozen or so other oxen and horses hitched to similar wagons. 'Tilda, anxious to get to her shopping, stood impatiently first on one foot, then on the other.

It took both of them to carry M'ma Chapelle's huge rush basket filled with eggs, and not until it was safely deposited on the counter of Bascom Brothers' General Store did Lance draw an easy breath.

"Eleven dozen, ye say?" inquired Bediah Bascom. "All the little pullet ones on the bottom, I suppose." But he grinned as he said it, and began lifting the eggs from the basket into a jerkin half full of sawdust.

'Tilda's black eyes were as big as pound sweets as she

walked slowly up and down the aisles. She picked her way among kegs of raisins, barrels of potash, and stacks of lamb skins with the wool still on, thinking what she would swap the eggs for if she hadn't been expressly told by her mother to exchange them for a bolt of calico.

Lance, whose lack of purchasing power seemed to him reason enough for not staring at merchandise he couldn't possibly buy, went outside. He was carrying under his arm the coffee mill with its broken handle, and his next errand was to find the whitesmith whose shop he had once visited with his father. It stood, if he remembered rightly, half way down the side street, around the corner from the Fish and Turtle Tavern.

But he forgot all about the whitesmith when, stepping down from the long, low porch that ran across the entire front of the store, he saw that something was going on near the Fish and Turtle. He couldn't make out what it was, but could see that a dozen or so men, and even several women with marketing baskets on their arms and children hanging to their skirts, were lined up on either side of the dusty road.

Clutching the coffee mill, Lance broke into a run.

"Hi, there, bub!" shouted someone. "Git off to one side. They're comin' your way!"

Lance, darting to the right from the very middle of the road, could now see that two horses, one a big rangy black, the other a small, dark bay, were restive under the reins of two drivers, each of whom was seated in a light, two-seated cart. In front of the horses someone had drawn, perhaps with the toe of his boot, a shallow furrough across the road.

" 'Tis eighty rods from that there line to Jake the Saddler's," volunteered a short little man at Lance's elbow. "I'm for Lawyer Bodycoat's big black. The bay is nothing but a farm horse, 'n a runt at that."

Lance silently nodded agreement. There didn't seem to be any room for argument on that score. He couldn't keep his eyes from the prancing black, whose feet pawed the ground and whose very nostrils appeared to be sniffing the victory that lay ahead.

"What are they waiting for?" he asked.

"See that fellow with the bald head holding his hat up? When he drops it, they'll be off. Watch now. There he goes. No—yes—he's dropped it!"

The next instant, horses and carts flew past Lance in a jumbled flash of hoofs and wheels, the drivers yelling and waving their whips. The crowd closed in behind in a smother of white dust.

The race was over by the time Lance, and he was among the first to arrive, had reached Jake the Saddler's. Someday, he was thinking, Cherry might grow into a fine, fast, handsome horse like this one of Lawyer Bodycoat's. Might even be a racer, too.

Then he forgot Cherry to stare with eyes wide and unbelieving. Everyone was crowding, not around the big black, but the little bay, and it was the bay's driver that Jake the Saddler was pounding on the back! Lance edged his way to within a foot of the winner who stood, sweated and trembling a little, but quite gentle under the many hands stretched out to stroke him.

Unlike Cherry, he hadn't a white hair on him. His legs, mane, and tail were black, his body and head deep bay. Like Cherry, however, he had small and exquisitely shaped feet. Like Cherry's too, his hair was soft and glossy, his eyes very dark, and his forehead broad.

"Who owns him?" asked Lance, looking about for the little man who had been his informant before, only to find that he had disappeared. Half-a-dozen eager voices, however, were ready to answer.

"He's rented out to Farmer Evans—"

"B'longs to a fellow lives over to Randolph—"

"Bob's usin' of him to clear fifteen acres heavy timber—"

"Owner took him for a bad debt—"

"Come up from somewheres in Massachusetts. Springfield, most likely—"

"Evans has the use of him for four bits a month—"

Reluctantly Lance reminded himself of the coffee mill to be repaired at the whitesmith's and of 'Tilda who was doubtless wondering what had become of him. With several backward glances at both horses and a final, lingering one, in which astonishment still mingled with admiration, for the little bay, he retraced his steps to turn down the lane beside the Fish and Turtle Tavern.

An hour later, he and 'Tilda, seated under a butternut tree on the grassy bank of the creek where they could watch the slow turning of the great dripping water

wheel, opened the lunch M'ma Chapelle had packed for
them. There were two mammoth hard-boiled duck eggs,
fried cakes put together with apple butter, and a tiny
stone jar of wild strawberry jam which they scraped
clean to the last crimson speck. To wind up with, there
was an inch cube of maple sugar for each from the spring
boiling-down. Lance thought it was the best meal he
had ever eaten, and even admitted as much to his companion.

'Tilda gave a scornful sniff. "You ought to see what
we'll have Thanksgiving! That is," she added as an after-
thought, "if my father does come back."

Lance remembered what Bediah Bascom had said
about P'pa Chapelle having an "itching foot," and wanted
to ask 'Tilda what he meant, but decided against it. Perhaps 'Tilda herself wouldn't know.

Afterwards they walked around a bit, with 'Tilda doing
a vast amount of window-shopping and Lance a vast
amount of thinking about the morning's race.

Slowly, store by store, they made their way to the
Fish and Turtle where sometime between noon and
sundown, according to Miller Robins, the Center Turnpike stage was due to stop. "It all depends," said he, "on
how many axles is broke on the Mountain, and iffen the
wash-out at Pierce's Corners is filled or not."

Lance was glad of the letter in his pocket and especially of M'ma Chapelle's instructions to deliver it to
no one but the stage driver. No matter how late the stage
arrived, he was in duty bound to wait for it.

"Don't be leaving it with that postmaster in the Tavern, Lance," she had warned him. "Chances are he'd ferget to put it in the sack at all. Know how to fix it? Write on it somewheres, best up in corner, whatever 'tis the driver makes yer pay. Most likely nearly two bits, seeing Uticy must be a lot more than a hundred miles from here."

One by one, and sometimes two by two, the entire population of Valley Mill, or so it seemed to Lance and 'Tilda, was gathering about the Tavern. That there was at least one passenger for the coach was shown by the tattered pennant, hoisted on a pole above the swinging wooden sign with its bright painting of something like a whale with a turtle on its back.

Idly, Lance scanned all the faces to detect anyone who seemed, by dress or baggage or air of importance, about to set out on adventure, but saw no one who filled the requirements.

Slowly the minutes went by, and he began to wonder just how long after all M'ma Chapelle would expect him to wait. There had been times, Miller Robins chuckled, when the old coach hadn't shown up until a whole day later than the one for which she was scheduled.

" 'Twill be dark long before we get home," he told 'Tilda.

"I don't mind," she said gaily. "And I'm sure Wash and Jeff won't."

Suddenly, even before Lance himself heard a sound, all heads turned to the north where the road curved with the creek. An instant later there was a roar and a rumble which grew louder and louder.

"Here she comes! Here she comes!" yelled the crowd.

And there she did indeed come, with a cloud of dust, a flourish of whip, shouts from the passengers with heads thrust out of the windows, and the clatter from the eight pairs of hoofs of four lathered horses. Squarely in front of the Fish and Turtle she rolled to a halt.

Simon Chittenden, the tavern keeper, famed for his bristly red whiskers, turned over his mail sack and picked up the one the driver tossed down. Several passengers clambered out to stretch cramped legs and exchange a word or two with the bystanders.

"—that spot o' clay this side o' Rutland Village—slick as pig's grease—"

"—looks like sure grit trouble in the Iron Works at East Bennington—"

"—iffen I was the President—"

Lance, intent on getting the driver's attention and transacting his little business about M'ma Chapelle's letter, forgot to watch for whatever Valley Mill resident was leaving home. Then, as he stepped back from the coach's wheel, he saw that a roughly dressed fellow with a cap of weasel fur pulled well down over his head, was limping out of the Tavern doorway and down the steps. It was not, however, the man's sallow face, his torn buckskin breeches, or even the fact that one of his jacket sleeves hung limp and empty which made Lance's eyes as large as a horned owl's at twilight.

It was the fact that the fellow was wearing a bandage below the knee of his right leg, and that the bandage was made of the towel from the peg beside the door of Lance's cabin!

Suddenly, as the man paused with one foot on the step of the stage and a hand on the door, he seemed to feel Lance's stare, turned his head, and saw him. Slowly his small green eyes narrowed, his mouth twisted. "Ye wouldn't," he whispered softly, bending toward him, "ye wouldn't, by any chance, be Mr. Busybody?"

The next moment he had entered the stage and slammed the door behind him.

Chapter IV

" 'Tis a threat to more than the peace of the Hollow."

"DID that dreadful-looking man with one arm and a hurt leg say something to you, Lance?" 'Tilda asked as they walked back to the grist mill.

Lance's expression was grim, but he had no intention of letting 'Tilda know the whole story. "He just asked me if I was somebody he thought he knew. I hope Miller Robins—"

"And were you?" persisted 'Tilda.

Lance stopped short in the road. "You do ask too many questions, 'Tilda Chapelle!" he said sharply. "Suppose I was. It isn't important, is it?"

'Tilda stopped too, and made funny little patterns in the dust with the toe of her shoe. Then she looked straight at Lance, her black eyes flashing, and spoke her mind.

"You think just because I'm a girl and three years younger than you be, that I've got no more sense than—than a want-wit sheep. I know very well that you and your pa and P'pa Chapelle used to be mighty excited about whatever 'twas going on in the Hollow of nights. I know you still hanker to find out, and I think that dreadful-looking man was just exactly like somebody who might be mixed up in something like that. As long as you won't tell me a single thing, I'll go down into the

42

Hollow myself some day and do my own discovering. I may be a girl—just what are you laughing at, Mr. Lance?"

For Lance was chuckling. "At you, 'Tilda . . . I mean at the thought of your traipsing about the Hollow. It's not any sort of a clearing, you know. There are gorges and swamps and windfalls likely to break both your legs, and there are bears and painters and probably mountain lions. Snakes, too . . . great long black ones. Don't talk nonsense. And here's the mill and I hope the meal is ready."

But Lance was not chuckling inside. He knew 'Tilda. I sure hope what I said will keep her away from the Hollow, he thought uneasily.

While Miller Robins loaded the bags of yellow meal into the back of the wagon, Lance gave one last look around for the little bay that had won the race. "Where does Bob Evans live?" he asked.

"Down the road a piece," replied the miller. "Nice little horse he tried out this morning. Seems sort of a pity now to use a high sperrited animal like that one just for clearing land."

"Yes," said Lance thoughtfully. "Yes, it does."

Wash and Jeff, after their long rest, stepped forth as briskly as oxen can and, once across the covered wooden bridge, were soon started on the long grade up the mountain.

"Why is a cover built over the bridge?" asked 'Tilda curiously. "Is it so horses won't be frightened at seeing the river and the mill wheel?"

Lance shrugged his shoulders. "I'm not sure I know, 'Tilda," he confessed. "Maybe it's to keep out the snow in the winter, but more likely it's to keep the bridge timbers from rotting. Why do *you* suppose it is?"

Now it was 'Tilda's turn to chuckle. "I think it's to make such a funny rumble and clatter when you drive through."

On both sides of the road the forest was already deep in twilight, and Lance knew it would be several hours before the Chapelle farm was reached. Oxen were all very well for ploughing, he reflected, but when it came to speed, just give him a horse like Cherry. Or that little bay.

'Tilda brought out two fried cakes left from lunch and gave one to Lance. She was eager to talk about all the sights she had seen that day, and for a long time chattered like a magpie without expecting a reply or, for that matter, giving Lance a chance to make one.

"It must be fun, Lance, to live where there are as many as twenty or twenty-one houses closer 'n three miles together. I do like that blue hat with a long feather. Some day I am going to have a two-wheeled cart and an enormous black horse exactly like the one that didn't win the race. I shall ride and ride and ride all up and down the State of Vermont. Wouldn't you just love to own a store filled with everything like Bascom Brothers? But perhaps you'll be a stagecoach driver, Lance. Weren't those passengers jammed in tight, though! If I had a two-wheeled cart and a big black horse and a blue hat with a long feather—"

Little by little, however, she grew less talkative and finally, "I think I'll climb into the back of the wagon," she announced, "and take a nap. A very, very short one because it's such fun to ride through the night. The stars 'n the moon 'n the screech owls 'n—'n—" She yawned sleepily, and soon Lance heard her making herself comfortable among the bags of meal and the bolt of red calico.

Lance was glad to be rid of 'Tilda's conversation, one-way though it was. It gave him the chance he wanted. The chance to think.

He knew now what had happened to his towel. The man who had boarded the stage had hurt his leg, probably on the way out of the Hollow. He had stopped in the clearing, perhaps to bathe the injury, and had found what would serve as a bandage hanging beside the cabin door. Curiosity, no doubt, had led him to look inside the cabin, and the sight of the telltale map had angered him into leaving the scrawled warning which Boney had all but destroyed.

The appearance of the man, whom 'Tilda so truly described as "dreadful looking," rooted more deeply than ever Lance's conviction that what went on in the Hollow needed investigation.

"Pa was sure dead right," he said to himself, "when he told me that whatever it is, 'tis a threat to more than the peace of the Hollow."

The monotonous plodding of the oxen, the complete darkness with which he was surrounded, the absence of any but occasional little night sounds, would, under ordinary circumstances, have lulled Lance into drowsiness. He could even have lain down on the seat and slept, knowing that Wash and Jeff would take them safely home. As it was, what with turning over and over his plans for the next day's exploring of the Hollow, he was still wide-eyed and alert when the oxen turned into the farm drive.

M'ma Chapelle and even the twins, who had bounced out of bed at the rumble of the wagon wheels, were waiting for them. There was rabbit stew, set aside to keep warm, and a pot of tea.

"Better stay here the night, Lance," M'ma Chapelle advised, after the oxen had been unyoked, fed, and let out into the pasture.

But Lance shook his head. "I must be home tonight. I'm rising early in the morning."

Mathilde, who had been very cross ever since she tumbled out of the wagon to find the ride was over and that she had slept most of the way, spoke up quickly. "I know what he wants to get up early for. He's going down into that awful Hollow."

Her mother gave Lance a quick look, started to speak, then apparently thought better of it.

Lance spent a few minutes in the lean-to, putting a fresh bandage on Cherry's leg, and replacing the old hay of her bedding with new. The swelling had lessened, and the flesh above and below the injury seemed cooler to the touch. For some reason, perhaps because of the darkness, Cherry submitted to Lance's ministrations less rebelliously than at any previous time.

Lance set out for the clearing with old Eagle-eye over one shoulder and a bag of journey-cakes, which M'ma Chapelle had made up for him during the day, over the other. The road through the woods was familiar enough to travel blindfold, even without the help of the moon which, riding high in the heavens, shed considerable light through the branches of the trees. But he was far sleepier than he had been in the wagon, and occasionally his feet stumbled from weariness. Never had the way seemed so long.

When he reached the crest of the hill near the fork, he sat down on the big rock to catch his breath after the climb. Through the gap in the forest, the moonlight was spreading a lake of silver mist across the valley below. He could hear the sound of many brooks flowing down to the creek.

I've half a mind, he thought, to lie down right here and take a nap.

He slid from the rock, placed Eagle-eye and the bag of journey-cakes on the ground beside him, stretched out full length on the dried leaves and pine needles, and closed his eyes.

Suddenly a sound which, in his drowsy state, he did not at first recognize for what it was, came to his ears. It was not the cry of an animal in pursuit of its prey, nor

the crashing of a dead branch from a distant tree. It was—
yes, it was unmistakably the sound of human voices.

Lance was instantly awake and sitting up, his head
cocked to one side. The voices were coming nearer.
Who would be abroad at this time of night? Would the
one-armed man with the wounded leg— But to think of
him was absurd. Long ago he must have reached Rutland
village, and there would be no stage back for several
days.

He realized that he could easily be seen in the moonlight by anyone passing within a few feet of the rock,
and crept into the shelter of the rock's shadow, pulling
the gun and bag after him. There he waited, ready to lift
his head cautiously for a glimpse of those to whom the
voices belonged as they went by.

To his keen disappointment the voices grew fainter
and then he could hear them no more. He knew what
had happened. The men had reached the fork and had
turned to the left instead of the right, taking the Ox
Road. The only place, moreover, from which they could
have come was the Hollow.

And if I could have seen them as they came over the
Ridge, thought Lance grimly, I'm sure they would have
been hunch-backed against the sky.

Hurriedly he rose to his feet, and once more shouldered
old Eagle-eye and the bag of journey-cakes. He was
eager to reach the clearing to find out if his belongings
were as he had left them.

Ten minutes later he opened the door of the cabin.

No one, so far as he could tell, had entered it. In the dim light he saw that the map was still on the wall. There were no scrawled sheets of paper visible, bearing threatening messages.

Standing old Eagle-eye in the corner beside his bunk, and emptying the sack of journey cakes into the big earthen jar out of reach of squirrels and chipmunks, he found himself yawning again and again. As he tumbled into bed, Lance made himself a sleepy promise.

"I'll look for footprints in the morning."

Chapter V

"Until the next full o' the moon."

LANCE rose later by several hours than he had planned. The many miles of riding back and forth to Valley Mill, the long walk home, the series of happenings during the day—all brought to him a heavy and dreamless slumber from which only the pangs of hunger finally waked him.

"Whew!" he exclaimed, as he saw how high the sun was in the sky. "And I need all the daylight I can get!"

Hardly stopping to wash the sleep from his eyes, he filled his pockets with as many of M'ma Chappell's journey-cakes as they would hold, took old Eagle-eye from the corner, and set out. "Looks as though a storm might be fixing," he murmured, "spite of that sun. All those clouds in the west."

At the fringe of woods he looked carefully for footprints in the ground made soft by the overflow from the trough, but didn't find any. Even those which had been left by the man with the wounded leg were gone now.

That part of the Hollow which lay between the clearing and the Ridge was all familiar to Lance. Both alone and with his father he had crossed and re-crossed it many times, sometimes in search of game, sometimes on what his father had called their "v'yages of exploration."

The going, until one came to the Ridge, was fairly easy. Lance's plan was simple: to reach Copper Coin Brook and there pick up the trail taken by the person who had dropped the coin which now, still shinier than any of its fellows, rested in his breeches pocket.

His eagerness to get to the brook put speed into his legs which the steep climb up the Ridge scarcely checked. He arrived at the top tired and thirsty, and, a few yards down the other side, turned from his path to drink from a spring he and his father had found long ago.

He was on his knees pushing away the leaves from the water's surface when a lumbering sort of crash in the bushes near by startled him. Gun in hand, he leapt to his feet. Not ten feet away, facing him, stood a beady-eyed, crooked-legged, inquisitive bear.

Lance put his gun to his shoulder, aimed for the spot between the button-size eyes, then dropped the gun to his side, flourished one arm, and uttered a yell, threatening, but not loud. With another cumbersome crash, the bear turned in its tracks and was off in the underbrush. "If I didn't have other business on my mind," Lance muttered under his breath, "you'd be dead bear by now!"

It's no use letting old Eagle-eye warn folks I'm in these parts, he was thinking. If it had been a painter now, 'twould have been different, but a harmless old bear—shucks!

He made quick time down the Ridge, but once at its foot was puzzled as to just which way to turn. In what direction did Copper Coin Brook actually lie? How had he come from it to the Ridge? For a long time he stood very still, staring about for any landmark which could guide him. He recalled that there had been a grove of white birch trees not very far from the spot where he had found the coin. If he could find that grove. . . .

He made several trial excursions in different directions, returning each time to his starting point. At the fourth attempt he came upon a small stream. Could it be the same one for which he was searching? He decided to follow it on the chance that it might prove to be Copper Coin Brook itself or a tributary running into the Copper Coin, and so ultimately bring him to the grove of white birch or to some other spot he would recognize.

For an hour Lance kept the stream in sight, even when it all but disappeared in a marsh, and once when it tumbled through a narrow gorge over rocks slippery and

green with moss. The farther he went without seeing one familiar scene, the more his heart sank.

When he did come suddenly upon the grove of white birch, he drew a deep sigh of relief. It *was* Copper Coin Brook itself which he had been following.

A few minutes later he reached the very place where the coin had lain. Now to find the trail along which the person who had dropped it there had come.

Taking off his boots, he waded to the other side. There he saw numerous prints of deer hoofs and many narrow deer runs, but nothing like a man-made path. Disappointed, even while reminding himself that on his previous visit he had been unable to find one, Lance plunged through the thickets first in one direction and then another. The only results were scratched face and hands, and a long tear in the sleeve of his jacket.

He was on the point of giving up when he saw something flash swiftly by in front of him, and knew he had startled a deer. He pushed through to where the deer had been an instant before, and, there at his feet, was what he had been looking for—a trail wide enough for two men walking abreast to follow. And it showed frequent use.

In his excitement over the discovery, he failed to note that the sunlight had disappeared and the sky was darkening overhead. One thought alone possessed him, and that was to follow the trail until it led him, as he was sure it would, straight into the heart of the Hollow and its mystery.

Yet even with this simple aim in mind he was balked at the very outset. In which direction should he go?

To place his compass points, he looked for the sun and for the first time became aware of the coming storm. Common sense urged him to be satisfied with what he had already accomplished, and to leave the following up of the trail to another day. To be caught in the Hollow in one of the torrential showers which often visited the region at this time of year would be a miserable experience.

Suddenly the thought jumped into his head that for once he didn't have to come to a decision. He had reached the spot where he now stood by so many roundabout ways that he had no idea in which direction the clearing lay. In the semi-darkness rapidly enveloping everything, it could easily be a long time before he found out where the trail was taking him, whether toward home or deeper into the Hollow. The thing to do was to get started.

He set out on a dog trot. The path twisted and turned and circled, dodging hills and swamps and once a small pond. Then it began to climb, but so gradually that Lance was not able to tell whether it was ascending the Ridge or not, although he had a feeling that it was. Sprinkles of rain came through the trees and he could hear the wind moving in great gusts in the branches above him. Occasional rumbles of thunder seemed to jar the very air.

The instant he came to the top of the Ridge he recognized the spot for what it was. Fire had swept over the summit at this point, and it was here that, for one brief moment, anyone would be visible against a lighted sky. It was here that he and his father had seen the two stooped men. With a fifty-fifty chance of choosing the direction toward the heart of the Hollow, he had taken the one leading away from it.

The mystery was still unsolved, but not for long, he vowed to himself. He would for the moment, storm or no storm, keep on until he learned at what place this end of the trail came out on the road on which last night he had heard voices. Tomorrow he would rise at dawn, retrace the portion of the trail he had covered today, and continue to the other end of it.

He stepped up the dog trot to a run. As he did so, a sound in the woods at his right startled him. He turned his head in its direction, and the next instant was sprawled on his stomach over the trunk of a tree across his path. All breath was knocked out of him, and for a moment he lay where he was without moving. When he did rise dizzily to his feet, he was too confused to trust his senses when he thought he heard exactly the same sound he had heard the night before—the sound of human voices.

As his mind cleared, however, he knew that he had been right. There *were* voices, and not very far away. Strangely, however, they were somewhere in the woods at his right, and not on the trail ahead.

Worming his way among the branches of the fallen maple, he lay concealed from any casual glance, yet in a position where, if the owners of the voices broke through to the trail within a reasonable distance, he could see them. As he waited, he reflected on the queerness of so nearly repeating last night's experience.

The voices were unmistakably coming closer, accompanied by the crackle of breaking underbrush. Lance's heart pounded as he wondered just how completely he was hidden by the maple leaves. It seemed to him that whoever was approaching was headed directly toward him. As a matter of fact, the first man to stride out of the woods struck the trail several yards from the spot where he lay, and in the semi-darkness Lance could see only that the man was short, and was wearing tall boots into which his breeches were tucked, a leather jacket, and a hat of some sort. What he called back to his companion was lost to Lance in the beat of the rain, now falling steadily.

The first words of the second man, however, reached Lance clearly enough. " 'Tis just as well there's no more o' this wearing your dang feet out 'til the next full o' the moon. Iffen you'd hark to the getting of a horse for this business—"

The rest of his complaining Lance didn't hear. Or, if he did, he heard it only with his ears and not at all with his brain. His mind was whirling. The second figure was limping badly, was wearing a cap of weasel fur, and had the same evil face as the person who had boarded the stage for Rutland Village. It couldn't, of course, be the same man. He couldn't, for one thing, have returned in so short a time from Rutland Village. But there was another, a surer reason. This man had two arms.

Long after both men had disappeared down the trail over which he had just come, Lance stayed where he was, waiting for the downpour to lessen and trying to make two and two add up to something more than three. When he finally set forth again, he was no nearer a solution.

"Only by finding out what these vagrants are really up to in the Hollow will I ever be able to figure it out," he reflected. " ' 'Till the next full o' the moon,' said the one who, yes, I know it was the one I saw taking the stage, two arms or not. ' 'Til the next full o' the moon.' That's when they'll be making another of these trips."

Presently another cause for speculation occurred to him. Why had the men chosen the hard going of the forest rather than the comparatively easy traveling of the trail? As a short-cut? But that would depend upon the spot from which they had come. Could it have been the clearing?

For a moment he was tempted to leave the trail himself, but immediately recognized the folly of doing so in the midst of a storm with night closing down. The memory of the bear he had frightened away came to him. It was one thing to meet a bear in daylight, and quite another to bump into him in the dark.

Sooner or later he was bound to hit Ox Road. The way might be twice as long, but it carried no risk of being lost, and once he was home there would be his warm bunk waiting for him and a fire on the hearth to dry his soaked clothes.

When at last, after what seemed many miles of up-and-down going, he found the ruts of Ox Road under his feet, he was sure he had never been so weary in his life. By the time he reached the fork and turned toward the clearing, he had ceased to think about anything but reaching the cabin. Nor had he noticed that the rain had stopped falling, and moonlight now and then spilled through remnants of ragged storm clouds.

A wave of relief swept over him as he came out of the woods.

But what had happened? Where was he? How could he have made such a blunder? This was not his clearing. It had no cabin on it.

A sudden puff of wind, gentle now that the storm was over, carried an acrid smell to his nose, at the same moment that a break in the clouds let through a flood of silver moonlight. In front of him the cabin he had helped his father build, the cabin which had been his home for three years, was a smoking pile of embers.

Chapter VI

"You'll get yourself killed, Mr. Lance!"

For a long time Lance stood where he was, staring at what that morning had been a sturdy, weather-proof building. After a while he sat down on the maple stump and wondered what to do next. How the cabin came to burn, he had no sure way of knowing. A spark from the hearth? a bolt of lightning? the two men he had seen emerging from the forest, who had given evidence with a threat of their dislike of his investigations in the Hollow? What difference did it make for the moment? The immediate fact to be faced was that he had no home, which meant no shelter.

He was cold, he was wet, he was weary in every muscle. He wanted a warm, dry spot where he could curl up and sleep.

He thought of the Chapelles, but dreaded the distance he must travel to reach them.

At last, however, he rose and, with one backward look,

set his tired feet upon the trail into the woods he had just left. When he reached the flat rock where ordinarily he rested, he kept doggedly on.

The Chapelle farm was dark, but Lance had no intention of rousing anyone. Not far from the lean-to was a huge stack of straw, the accumulation of several years. From it he had pulled Cherry's bedding. Now he burrowed at its base until he had fashioned a hole deep and wide enough to crawl into. It wasn't especially soft, but it was warm and dry and safe. As he closed his eyes he heard a slight stirring and whinny from the lean-to. Only Cherry knew of his presence.

It was Boney who waked him, sniffing and snapping at his boots as they protruded from the bottom of the stack. It was the twins, attracted by Boney's excited yipping, who carried the news into the sunny kitchen that somebody was "a-hiding in the straw pile," and it was Mathilde who recognized the boots and the long legs to which they were attached. Lance, only half-aroused, was trying to kick Boney away.

"Whatever are you doing in our straw heap, Lance?"

Lance, crawling out and blinking in the bright sunlight, told her sleepily, while Mathilde's black eyes grew round and big.

"Whatever are you going to do now?"

Lance told her that, too, reaching a decision on the spur of the moment. "Get me a job in the iron works."

Mathilde's eyes grew even bigger. "Come, tell Ma," she said. "I'll dish you up some corn mush."

Lance, brushing bits of straw from his clothes and his neck and his hair, followed her, thinking with considerable satisfaction that his quick, unconsidered answer had indeed been a good one. He would do just that; get a job until he earned enough money to live on while he rebuilt his cabin so that he could keep on ferreting out the mystery of the Hollow.

M'ma Chapelle was not in the kitchen and the wooden sink was filled with unwashed dishes.

"Ma's down with the fever," said Mathilde briefly. "She's in the bedroom yonder."

Lance tiptoed to the door of the one room opening from the kitchen, and saw M'ma Chapelle turn a flushed face toward him from her pillow.

"So glad you came," she murmured. "So glad you came. Better stay a spell. You can sleep overhead. 'Tilda will help you with the chores. There's a new calf to bring up from the pasture. Better look to Cherry's leg again. There's turnips to be fetched to the root cellar. You will stay a spell, won't you?"

"Yes," said Lance slowly. "Yes, I'll stay." Always those Chapelles!

Perhaps M'ma Chapelle was aware of his reluctance. "It's—it's only until 'Tilda's father comes back. Should —should be here any day now." She sighed and closed her eyes.

A strange, new life began for Lance. It was, on the whole, not an unpleasant one, in spite of those frequent moments when he felt that he was wasting time he could have used to further his own plans. He yearned to return to the Hollow, but there was no chance to do so. There was always so much to be done.

There was wood to be chopped, there were fences to be mended, hill after hill of potatoes to be dug and stored; the foundation of the house had to be banked with sweepings from the barn, against the cold of winter. And day in and day out there were the regular chores—milking, watering and graining the stock, butter making, tending the fire. Sometimes Mathilde could and did help, but she had her own work in caring for M'ma Chapelle and the twins, in getting meals, and in keeping the house clean.

One thing, however, Lance promised himself. When the full moon came again, he would forsake the Chapelles long enough to lie in wait at the point where the trail from the Hollow came out upon the Ox Road, until he saw those strange men and learned the secret of their trips.

In the meantime, Lance found not having to get his own meals very agreeable. Mathilde wasn't as good a cook as her mother, but she could mix up a batter of buckwheat for griddlecakes to be eaten with maple syrup which were a heap sight more appetizing than a steady diet of dry journey cakes. There was still wild cherry preserve left over from last winter's batch, and Lance himself, under the invalid's direction, made three loaves of bread and a pan of biscuits to go with them. Mathilde admitted grudgingly they were almost as good as M'ma Chapelle's.

In contrast with his solitary days on the clearing, Lance

liked being part of a family. Even the twins were good company when they weren't up to monkeyshines, or getting under foot, or forgetting to shut the door of the chicken house. There were actually hours at a stretch when he could endure 'Tilda. They were, however, often far apart, and not when she was in one of her teasing moods.

"You ought to be a nurse. Fussing over a horse so."

"Who do you 'spose set fire to your old cabin? I think prob'bly you were just happy-go-lucky careless, like Ma says I am, and put on too many pine knots to once, and they blazed too much and made a chimney fire."

"Better cut your hair, Mr. Lance Long Locks. You look for sure like those Dorrilites Pa and I saw in Valley Mill. Hair clear to their shoulders and beards two-three feet long."

But she mended the tear in the sleeve of his jacket, saw that the corn mush or oat porridge was ready when he came in from the morning chores, and sometimes forgot to chatter.

Before two weeks had passed, Lance's happiest moments came to be those after the night's chores were done, the twins had gone to bed, and Mathilde was busy with making her mother comfortable for the night. Then, with a bit of old blanket for a saddle in one hand and a bridle in the other, he would go hopefully down to the pasture. There Cherry, at last rid of her bandage and not limping at all, would be waiting at the bars for the lump of brown sugar which Lance saved each morning instead of using it to sweeten his corn mush.

Cherry had accepted Lance as a friend, but not as a rider. The very sight of the blanket and bridle was enough to send her galloping as far as the Little Pasture on the top of the hill. Lance had to hide them in a clump of bushes and stalk the colt as though she were a deer before he could get within ten feet of her. Cherry also had a wicked way of flinging up her heels at unexpected moments, and Lance soon learned to approach her with caution.

Lance's determination to ride Cherry was backed by an idea which had come to him soon after his arrival at the Chapelle farm. Before that time, when his days were free from any particular occupation, the miles he tramped into the Hollow and back, and between the cabin and the farm, had been nothing more than fun and good exercise. Now, however, night found him too weary to contemplate even covering the distance to the spot where the trail joined Ox Road, much less following the men and finding out what their destination was when they left the Hollow on their periodic excursions.

If, however, he could ride Cherry, the scheme he had in mind for the next full o' the moon would stand a better chance of being successfully carried out.

But as the days went by and Cherry, eager enough to nuzzle the lump of sugar from Lance's hand, still shied suspiciously at any glimpse of the bridle, Lance decided he would have to enlist the help of Mathilde whether he wanted to or not.

He outlined a plan one morning as he and Mathilde and the twins were eating breakfast in the sunny kitchen. "I'll get Cherry quite used to taking sugar from you the way she does from me, and while she's doing it, I'll just slip the bridle right over her head. When she doesn't mind the bridle being on, I think she'll let me ride her. After a while anyhow."

But Mathilde wasn't interested. "I don't see why you want to ride her," she said indifferently. "You'll only fall off."

Lance persisted. "You don't have to see why. But maybe you will some day. Maybe it's very important for you and your ma and pa that I do learn to ride her."

Mathilde looked thoughtfully out of the window toward the distant valley. "Going to ride her down into the Hollow?" she asked.

Lance was glad to give "No" as a reasonably truthful answer.

'Tilda gave no sign of being convinced, but she was plainly more attentive. "I think it's a very silly idea," she said finally. "If you'll help with the churning, though, and the supper dishes so I'll be through earlier, why, perhaps I will, although I'm not out-and-out promising."

Lance, bent now on securing her assistance, did more than help with the churning and the supper dishes. He mixed up the buckwheat batter for next day's griddle cakes, carried M'ma Chapelle's tray to her, and even put

the twins to bed. Mathilde, he saw to it, had no excuse whatever for not doing what he asked of her.

The afterglow of a rose-and-gold sunset colored the sky as Lance and Mathilde tramped through the truck patch, crossed the brook on flat stepping-stones and so came to the pasture. Cherry, grazing some distance away, sauntered over slowly for her sugar. When she saw that Lance was not alone, she stopped a few feet from the fence, and threw up her sleek little head.

"Stand right still, 'Tilda!" cautioned Lance. "Here, Cherry! Come on, Cherry! Here's your sugar!"

The colt moved slowly to take the sugar from Lance's outstretched palm. With his free hand Lance stroked the smooth glossy patch between Cherry's ears. "Hold out your sugar now, 'Tilda," he said softly.

Mathilde put forth her hand. Cherry rolled her eyes, snorted, seemed about to back away, apparently thought better of it, and helped herself to a second lump.

"Pat her forehead a bit, the way I did," whispered Lance. Cherry submitted to that also.

"Tomorrow night I'll try to put the bridle on," said Lance. "This is enough for now."

Mathilde stared at him. "You mean you want me to keep on coming down here night after night—"

"Oh, 'Tilda!" Lance's voice was impatient. "Gentling a colt isn't a thing you can do in a hurry, especially a colt with lots of spirit like Cherry. It takes time and persistence and—and, well, persistence."

"You'll get yourself killed, Mr. Lance," declared Mathilde. "You'll just get yourself good and killed." She turned back toward the farmhouse.

"If you won't help, I'll keep on by myself," retorted Lance stubbornly. "I'm going to make Cherry let me ride her before"—he started to say, "the next full moon" but changed it to, "well, just as soon as I can."

Mathilde sniffed and, perhaps because she was holding her nose so very high in the air, did not see the root of an old wild apple tree hooped along the ground in front of her. Catching her toe on it, she sprawled headlong.

Lance hauled her quickly to her feet. "Trying to break a leg, 'Tilda?"

But Mathilde, brushing the dirt and dead leaves and bits of twigs from her dress, refused to answer, and the two walked the rest of the way home in silence.

Chapter VII

"Is—is there a letter?"

SLOWLY M'ma Chapelle recovered from the fever until at last she was able to sit up for a few minutes each day. But she continued to look pale and thin, and worried, too.

There came a morning when she had Mathilde call Lance in from the truck patch where he was forking up the last of the potatoes, throwing those of a certain size into one pile and all the nuggins, which would go to Amanda the sow, into another. Lance was glad of the summons. He was hot and thirsty and his back ached, and he had been telling himself he never wanted to see another potato. After a long, cool drink of water from the spring, he hurried into the house.

M'ma Chapelle, who would not get up until afternoon, made him sit down in the wooden rocker at the foot of her bed.

"Lance, I've had a-plenty time lying here so long to think things over," she began. "Winter is coming on and plans for it must be made. Looks like a hard one, too, from the amount o' down 'Tilda says she's getting from the ducks. And an early one. Wild geese went over again last night. If 'Tilda's pa shouldn't be back—I mean, if anything's a-happened to him—you can't stay on. 'Tisn't right you should, wanting to get started on a job in the iron works. If 'tweren't for this sickness, well, 'Tilda and I could manage. As 'tis—

"This is what I want you to do. Drive Wash and Jeff to Valley Mill. Find out at the Fish 'n Turtle if there's a letter for me. There's been time enough for an answer to the one I sent. If there is, bring it back. If not, well, in that case I want you to take the stage to Rutland Village."

Lance's eyes grew as big as Mathilde's when she was surprised. Rutland Village! Why, that was all of forty miles away! "What am I to do in Rutland Village, ma'am?" he asked eagerly.

M'ma Chapelle folded her thin hands on top of the Irish chain bedquilt. "I have a second cousin there. Her name is Dilsie Buell and she lives in a house two doors from the courthouse. There'll be zinnias in the front yard. Tell her what has happened. Ask her iffen she'll take in 'Tilda and the twins and me over the winter. She's the only folks I have."

"How about the stock, ma'am, if you have to leave the farm?" asked Lance slowly.

M'ma Chapelle sighed. "We'll face that trouble when it

comes to us, Lance. I'm going to believe there'll be a letter at the Fish 'n Turtle."

"When shall I go?"

"Tomorrow. I figure that's the day for the stage."

Lance made rapid calculations. If he did indeed go to Rutland Village and had to wait there several days for the return trip of the stage, would he be back in time to carry out his own plans when the moon was full? Would there be enough days left in which to gentle Cherry before he needed to use her? There won't be too much leeway, he thought to himself.

He jumped to his feet. There was plenty to do to make the carrying on of the farm easier for Mathilde during his absence.

M'ma Chapelle lay back against the pillow and closed her eyes. "Better leave by sunup," she murmured. "If so be you have to go to Rutland Village, you musn't miss the stage."

That very evening Lance rode Cherry for the first time.

He had put in a day so crowded with extra chores that he hadn't once thought about his nightly visit to the pasture. Then, suddenly, everything that could be done was done. A dozen seasoned logs from the woodshed were rolled into the kitchen, ready for the fire upon the hearth. The rest of the winter vegetables were stored in the root cellar. The sow's pen and the chicken house were cleaned out. Fresh straw was laid for the cow with the new born calf.

Mathilde, in addition to her tasks indoors, would have to feed the stock and milk the cows, but that was all.

"It's quite enough!" she had declared, being much annoyed because she could not go with Lance. "You just better believe, Mr. Gadabout Lance, that if Ma weren't sick, I'd never let Wash and Jeff go one step out of this yard without me along. Why, I've never in all my life been to Rutland Village!" But she grumbled only to Lance, and not once within her mother's hearing.

She refused to go to the pasture, and Lance had the glory and the fun of mounting Cherry with no assistance whatever, except from those tempting lumps of brown sugar.

The sun had set behind the hills before Lance was free to leave the house, and the soft purple twilight was falling rapidly. Lance hid the bridle in a clump of sumac bushes, then, with the sugar, coaxed Cherry near them. Somehow, perhaps because of the dusk which rendered objects indistinct, he caught the colt off guard, and had the bridle on before Cherry knew what was happening.

Instantly the little creature became all flashing heels, tossing head, and flaring nostrils. She reared, she plunged, she waltzed.

"Now, Cherry girl—now, Cherry—" Lance wheedled and coaxed, but Cherry would have none of him.

After what seemed hours, she came to earth for a brief space to stand quite still, spent and trembling. In that split-second, Lance forgot all about his intention to gentle the little creature by degrees. Impulsively he leapt to her back.

Cherry, taken by surprise, remained motionless for an instant, but an instant only. Then she rocketted to her hind feet. Lance gripped the bridle straps with both hands, pressed his knees deep into the colt's flanks, shut his eyes, and hung on for dear life. For a wild moment, he felt a dizzy sense of violent speed. Then he was lying on the ground a dozen yards from the spot where he had been, and Cherry, bridle and all, was madly off to the Little Pasture on the top of the hill.

"I *did* ride her! I *did* ride her!" exulted Lance, as he rose and limped after the fleeing colt. "I rode her and perhaps next time she won't mind so much. And I won't either," he added ruefully, rubbing his thigh which had struck a rock when he fell.

It was dark before Lance finally caught up with Cherry and managed, after many tries, to recover the bridle. Fortunately, the skies were clear and the starlight bright enough to guide him down the hill, across the pasture, over the brook, and through the truck patch to the house.

"I guess you just went and forgot you're rising at sunup, Mr. Lance!" Mathilde greeted him. Lance stared at her. Mathilde was quite right. He *had* forgotten.

The sun was bright in the east when Wash and Jeff turned out of the drive into the grassy road. Lance, bundled against the chill of dawn with a heavy horse blanket round his knees and an old brown tippet of P'pa Chapelle's tied down over his cap about his neck and ears, was still yawning and trying sleepily to recall the different things M'ma Chapelle had told him he must, and must not, do.

"Go to the Fish 'n Turtle and ask about the letter—iffen so be you have to go to Rutland Village, leave the team at Farmer Evans'—iffen Dilsie shouldn't be to home, hunt her at the neighbors—don't miss the stage back—"

His stage fare was wrapped in a bit of linsey-woolsey and tucked far down into his breeches' pocket. There was a second letter, too, to be sent to Uticy telling of M'ma Chapelle's plans in case no word did come from her husband.

"I sure hope I do everything straight," worried Lance. "Call at the tavern and ask for a letter for Mrs. Pierre Chapelle—if there isn't any letter, leave Wash and Jeff at Farmer Evans'—"

A sudden thought brought him wide awake. "Farmer Evans—why, he must be the Bob Evans who's a-renting the bay that won the race. Maybe I'll get to see that little horse again!"

The miles to Valley Mill seemed to Lance longer than before, and by the time he reached the covered bridge he was convinced his own two legs were five times as speedy as the four of any slow-poke ox. Part of the time he slept, and part he spent planning what he would do when the moon was full. The rest of the time he had sat idly holding the reins and dreaming how someday he would own a horse like Cherry or the little bay. If there was a letter at the tavern saying P'pa Chapelle would soon be home, he could leave those Chapelles as soon as he cleared up the mystery in the Hollow. Then he would get a job in the Iron Works, and could save his money and buy such a' horse and—and— The rumble of the wagon wheels on the bridge broke in on his dream.

Lance halted Wash and Jeff before the tavern, unwound the brown tippet, and climbed down from his seat. It was good to be on his feet after the long ride. He stood still for a moment, stretching his arms, and looking up and down the quiet street. There was no one in sight.

He stared at the tavern door with its huge iron hinges. Should he knock with his fist or try the latch and, if it yielded, walk in?

The problem was solved when suddenly the door was opened from within and the innkeeper himself, leather apron, rolled-up sleeves, and long Dutch pipe, stood on the threshhold.

He looked Lance up and down, took his pipe out of his mouth, put it back, and spoke between puffs, in chopped off sentences. "Drivin' for Chapelles again. Expect you're livin' there. Good thing. Gettin' out o' that Hollow. Place is hanted. Expect you're meetin' the stage. Not due for two hours. Won't be here for four. Nice day. Not too cold. Not too warm."

Lance swallowed. So much of his own fate seemed to him to depend on the answer he was about to get from the question he was going to ask. "Is—is there a letter here for Mrs. Pierre Chapelle, Mr.—Mr.—"

"Name's Chittenden. Simon Chittenden. Same as my

father. Fell at Saratogy. A letter, now. Don't remember none. I'll take a look. Come in. Sit down."

Lance followed him into a high-ceilinged room with huge beams, a long fireplace over which a small roasting pig on a spit was slowly turning, and a dozen or so pine tables with benches on one of which he sat down. Simon dropped to his knees behind the counter to rummage among the shelves.

After what seemed a very long time, the innkeeper rose to his feet, brushing his knees. "No, sir. No letter. Didn't remember none. Could come on today's stage. 'Taint likely. Important?"

Lance nodded.

"Too bad. From that vagrant Pierre, I expect. Goes land-hunting 'mong the Yorkers. Got a farm o' his own. Here in Vermont. Fourteenth state o' the Union. No better country in God's universe."

Again Lance nodded, but he was hardly aware of what Simon was saying as he wondered just what to do next. In spite of the innkeeper's doubts, there was still a possibility of the letter's arriving on the stage. If it didn't, however, he must board the coach at once, and there would be no opportunity to make arrangements about Wash and Jeff.

"I'll take care of them now," he decided, "and if the letter should come I'll get them again."

He stood up. "How do I find Farmer Evans?" he asked.

"Bob Evans?" The innkeeper puffed a minute on his long pipe. "Lives beyant the bridge. On the left. First place ye come to. Ever see that hoss o' hisn? Smartest little hoss ever laid eyes on. Goin'? See you later. Stage comes. Iffen it comes."

Lance was climbing up to his seat again when he heard Simon's voice behind him. "I say, lad!"

Lance paused with one foot on the floor of the wagon, the other on a spoke of the great front wheel. "I say, lad!" Simon Chittenden had left the stone step of the tavern and walked down the path to the wagon. "I just remembered. Man with one arm. Weasel skin hat. Was asking for you. Know him?"

Lance swung himself up to the seat and picked up the reins. "Not exactly," he said. "Not exactly, but I'm a-going to."

Chapter VIII

"You should have come yesterday."

I T was a very fortunate thing, reflected Lance, as he bounced over the Otter Creek Highway, that the Center Turnpike Stagecoach Company put strong leather straps into its vehicles for passengers to hang on to. Also, that it didn't really make any difference at all that the windows were both small and dirty, for what could anybody see in the whirling cloud of white dust kicked up by four pair of galloping hoofs? And furthermore, at the mad rate they were going, they would certainly reach Rutland Village in two hours rather than the five the handbill posted on the Tavern wall promised.

All of these thoughts occurred to Lance during the first few minutes he was inside the coach, and in regard to only the last one did he at any time change his mind.

The stage had been late, as Simon Chittenden, the innkeeper, had prophesied it would be, and Lance had had ample time to drive Wash and Jeff to Farmer Evans' and make arrangements for their keep during his absence. Bob himself had not been at the farmhouse, but his wife had told Lance where to find him.

"He's a-clearing of the last piece along the edge o' the swamp. Not that I can't answer for his being willing to take your team while you're gone. But you know how a man is. Likes to run hisself. Besides, he is allus hankering to have a body drop in to cheer him on. Clearin' the primeval forest outen your back yard is a chore."

"Yes, ma'am," Lance had nodded, remembering how hard he and his father had worked on their own little clearing. "I know."

Taking the direction indicated by the woman's pointed finger, Lance found not only the farmer but the little bay horse as well. At the moment Lance broke through a grove of yellow-trunked aspens, the bay was snaking over the uneven ground a twelve foot spruce log nearly the thickness of his own chunky body.

Lance explained his errand.

"Sure thing," said Farmer Evans. "Leave 'em as long as convenient to ye." He saw Lance's eyes on the horse and called out a "whoa!" The little bay stopped obediently. "I sure wish I owned that animal," said Farmer Evans wistfully. "Handsome, isn't he?"

"Can't you buy him, Mr. Evans?" Privately Lance was thinking that, if he were Bob Evans, he'd sell the whole farm, if necessary, in order to buy that little horse.

The farmer shrugged his shoulders. "Owner won't sell. Music teacher he is. Lives over to Randolph. Don't need a powerful creature like this one any more'n I need his fiddle. He's just pig-headed. But someday I'll buy him. Some day I'll offer a sum too big to refuse!"

"Someday I'll buy him!" The words rang in Lance's ears as he walked back to the tavern. They roused in him a determination to get a job the very minute he was rid of the responsibility of those Chapelles so that he too could say with reasonable hope of fulfillment, "Some day I'll buy a horse, too!"

He had been the only person to board the stage from Valley Mill, and the driver had obligingly waited while Simon Chittenden opened the mail pouch to make sure no letter from Pierre Chapelle had arrived at the very last moment.

When he climbed inside, however, he found six other passengers, three men and two women, one of whom was holding a child. The air was warm and stuffy, and smelled of snuff and woollen garments and cheese and peppermint candy. The heat at once made Lance drowsy, and he wondered if he would fall asleep. After a few moments, what with the up-and-down bounces whenever the coach went over a thank-ye-marm, and the violent sidewise movements whenever it dodged a hole or slewed around a corner, he no longer worried about staying awake, but only how to keep himself out of the laps of the other passengers and keep them out of his.

A jolt which exceeded anything that had gone before brought forth a mild comment from the man in black woollen breeches, yellow waistcoat, and long green coat with yellow buttons on it, who sat between the other two men on the seat opposite Lance. "Seems like they ought to have got that there quagmire filled by now."

"Might as well build a log causey and be done with't," grunted the man on the speaker's right, who wore faded blue nankeen breeches and a black waistcoat with white stripes. A black coat lay across his knees, and his white shirt sleeves were ruffled at the wrists.

The third man folded a pair of plump hands on top of the round wooden cheese box he held on his lap. "This isn't too bad, brother, on this stretch. Wait till ye get to Clarendon Crossing where the washout was. Iffen we don't break an axle there, 'twill mean the Lord is watching over us special. I've had two axles broken under me already at that same identical spot."

As it happened, the driver, when he arrived at Clarendon Crossing, took no chances. He reined his horses to a halt, climbed down from his high seat, flung open the door.

"All inside outside," he ordered. "Outside, and lend a hand."

Lance was glad to fill his nostrils with fresh air, and cheerfully took his place at one of the big wheels to help ease the great awkward body of the coach down into, and up out of, the broad gully, while the driver stood at the heads of the front pair of horses and kept them from breaking into a mad gallop. The two women, daintily holding their long petticoats clear of the mud, stayed well in the rear until the coach was across. The child, a fat little boy in a blue velvet suit, hid shyly behind his mother.

Lance could see that the highway was entering a pass and that a steep and winding grade lay ahead, also that the road was of clay and in many places appeared to be both wet and slippery.

"I can understand now why the coach takes so long to get anywhere," he reflected, as he stepped from stone to stone through the gully, "and why it is more often late than on time."

Twice more the stagecoach stopped. Once to leave the woman and child at a tiny cabin set amidst tall, bushy pines, and once while the driver carefully examined the hoof of each one of the four horses for loose stones picked up in their frogs. There had been a breath-catching moment on the down grade the other side of the mountain when the horses had had trouble keeping their footing on the soapy clay. The woman with the child had screamed, and the man with the round cheese box on his lap and ruffled sleeves had closed his eyes and moved his lips. Lance had pressed the soles of his feet hard against the floor, and drawn a sigh of relief when the foot of the mountain was reached and the level floor of the Otter Creek Valley stretched ahead.

The afterglow of a bright sunset was fading from the sky when at last the horses, spurred partly by the knowledge that supper was at hand and partly by a flick of the long bull snake of the driver who fancied a bit of a flourish at the end of his run, galloped into Rutland Village.

Lance, who couldn't help feeling excited, climbed out hurriedly and glanced around, his eyes widening in surprise. Why, Rutland Village was a city!

The main street was three times as long as that of Valley Mill, with six times as many buildings on it. From where he was standing in front of Mead's Inn, which would have made two of the Fish and Turtle, he could see the whole business section. There were three meeting-houses, several stores, one with a big sign in front of it lettered "Printing Office," and a tiny square stone structure with bars across its one window which could be nothing else than the town jail.

The street faced a narrow green, on the opposite side of which were several small frame houses and a large oblong building imposing enough to be the County Courthouse. Two doors from this M'ma Chapelle had said her cousin, Dilsie Buell, lived.

Lance had two good reasons for wanting to reach Dilsie Buell's home as soon as possible. One was that the sooner he could shift his responsibilities for the Chapelle family the freer he would be to think about his own future. The other was a more immediate motive, urging him to hurry across the little green. M'ma Chapelle had told him that Dilsie would lodge him for the time which must pass before the stage returned to Valley Mill, and had added, "She makes the rarest bear meat stew I ever tasted. Puts down her own bear steaks every summer. Just mention I said so."

Bear meat stew, Lance felt, now that the jouncings of the stage coach were over, was just what he would like above everything else.

The first thing Lance noticed when he came up to the

stone wall which ran in front of the house was that the zinnias had been caught by frost. Their leaves hung limp from the blackened stalks, and the once bright flowers were shrivelled and faded. But the fact that they were there at all gave Lance confidence that he was knocking at the right door when he lifted the circlet of wrought iron and let it fall. Once he knocked, and then, as no one came in answer, he knocked again. And yet again.

He listened intently, but could hear no sound from within. Stepping back, he stared up at the top of the huge square chimney around which the house was built. Not the tiniest wisp of smoke was coming out of it. M'ma Chapelle's cousin, Dilsie Buell, was all too plainly not at home. The next step was to find out when she would be back.

Lance looked toward the house nearest to Dilsie's. It stood within its own stone wall a hundred or so yards away. There was plenty of life there. Two barking dogs, a woman bringing in clothes from a hempen rope hung between two maple trees, and a dozen or more children, scampering madly about in the deepening twilight, took the edge off the sudden feeling of loneliness which had swept over him.

As he turned from Dilsie's and walked toward the noisy yard, the woman, her arms filled with garments, came to meet him.

"I've come to see Miss Dilsie Buell," explained Lance. "I've come from Valley Mill."

The woman stared at him. "For the lands' sake!" she

exclaimed, as children and dogs gathered about her. "For the very land's sake! All the way from Valley Mill! But you should have come yesterday. Dilsie's gone to Hazen's Notch to housekeep for her brother. Left last night and won't be back till sugarin' time."

Lance's heart dropped to the soles of his feet. Here was something he had not foreseen, and surely M'ma Chapelle had not foreseen it either, for she had given no instructions as to what to do in such circumstances. However would she and 'Tilda and the twins manage now for the winter? For that matter, what would he do himself until the day after tomorrow when the stage, if nothing interfered with its schedule, would be going back to Valley Mill?

His troubled thought kept him from saying anything at all for a moment.

"You've journeyed a right long way," said the woman sympathetically. "Come on in and sit down a spell."

Lance, still too bewildered at this unexpected turn of events to do otherwise than accept the invitation, made his way between dogs and children, into a warm, neat kitchen with candles already lighted on the mantel above the fireplace.

"We've all et an hour back," said the woman, "but there's always tea, and it so happens I've a fresh batch o' bread and churning of butter. You'll feel better for something in your insides."

The cup of hot, strong tea and the thick slice of dark, grainy, molasses-sweetened bread seemed as welcome to

Lance as bear meat stew would have been. As he ate, the children turned somersaults on the floor and the dogs yelped and nipped at their heels. The woman, paying no heed to either children or dogs, sprinkled and folded and piled, on the other end of the long pine table at which Lance sat, the clothes she had brought in from the line.

Lance was trying hard to think what to do next, and reflecting that he would have felt less at a loss overtaken by night in the depths of the Hollow than here among so many persons, all provided with their own shelter.

Doubtless the woman knew what was puzzling him. "I wish I could lodge you for the night," she said slowly. "There are so many of us. We sleep like peas in a pod. But maybe—"

Her words brought Lance to a quick, impulsive decision. He swallowed the last crumb of bread and rose to his feet. "Thank you, ma'am," he said earnestly. "But I already have a place to stay. Mead's Tavern. I'm putting up for the night at Mead's Tavern."

Chapter IX

"Come clean, Sonny, or else—!"

ONCE Lance had left behind the warm and friendly
kitchen and was scuffing through the crisp leaves
that carpeted the green, he began to question the wisdom
of his sudden decision to spend the night at the Inn. Such
an act had been no part of M'ma Chapelle's plan. Neither,
for that matter, had Cousin Dilsie's going to Hazen Notch
to housekeep for her brother.

He had in his pocket the money for the return fare
on the stage, but the sum would not cover both his pas-
sage and his meals and lodgings for two nights. If, on the
other hand, he used it for a good night's rest at the
tavern and a packet of journey-cakes, he felt confident
of being able to rise at dawn and cover on foot the many
miles which lay between Rutland Village and Valley Mill.
The journey would take the better part of two days and
mean one night spent in a haymow or under a straw heap.
However, that prospect did not daunt him any more
than did the thought of the walk itself, and he was confident of reaching Valley Mill soon after, if not actually
before, the stage itself.

The only part of the scheme which he disliked was
that which faced him now—presenting himself at Mead's
Inn. All such places, he had gathered from P'pa Chapelle,
were rough and rowdy, filled with wagoners and card

sharps, who stayed up all night playing Hi-Lo Jack and drinking enormous flaggons of rum noggin. Moreover, according to the same source, these roisterous persons had a fancy for making the butt of crude, practical jokes any stranger who happened along. Perhaps he would do better to curl up under one of the maples on this very green.

He stood still for a moment to wonder how he, who had been finding it hard ever since his father died, to make up his mind about anything, had just done it so quickly. "I'm putting up for the night at Mead's Tavern." That was exactly what he had said.

He glanced up at the twinkling stars overhead. Their very brightness promised a sharp night. Sleeping on the green would be a shivering affair. Also, there was that little stone jail standing so handily a few yards away for any vagrants picked up by the constable. Getting himself arrested wasn't a part of M'ma Chapelle's plans either.

"Hi, there!"

Lance turned on his heel to face the queerest-appearing person he had ever laid eyes on, a man of an astonishing leanness, long beak of a nose, hair which hung to his shoulders and looked, in the darkness, to be red. A collection of odd garments fluttered about his frame in the night breeze, and a scrap of cloth hat with a feather in it clung to the back of his head.

"Hi!" returned Lance, doubtfully.

"Stranger?"

"Yes," said Lance. "Are—are you?"

"Not in a manner of speaking, as you might say. Got my own little place on the outskirts." He waved a loose-jointed hand in an indefinite direction. "Fixed for the night?"

"I'm staying at Mead's Tavern," said Lance.

Hardly were the words out of his mouth, before the man grabbed his scrap of hat from his red locks, pressed it against his chest, and bowed very low. "I crave your pardon, sir. I shorely crave your pardon. I didn't surmise I was addressing tavern company." The next instant he had vanished in the darkness. Two minutes later Lance had completely forgotten him.

The first greeting Lance had from the tavern as, hesitantly, he pushed open the heavy door, was a rush of warm, smoky air. There were the mingled smells of roasting meat, smouldering logs, the steamy woollen clothing of a score of men seated on benches at half-a-dozen tables or standing in groups in front of the vast fireplace.

The second greeting was a tired, "Your wish, sir?" from a sad-looking person with a white apron tied about his middle.

"I want a room for the night," said Lance.

The sad-looking person turned to the others. "He wants a room for the night," he announced softly.

"He wants a room for the night!" bellowed a man at one of the tables, and banged a fist down so heavily that the tankard out of which he had been drinking jumped two inches and spilled some of its contents.

And suddenly it seemed to Lance as if everyone in the

Inn and even the very rafters themselves were shouting in unison, "He wants a room for the night—wants a room for the night—room for the night—"

Then everything was as quiet as it had been noisy.

"I can let you have a third of a bed," said the sad-looking person, "for four bits."

A third of a bed! The bed to be shared, no doubt, with two of the assembled company here before his eyes. Lance's heart sank, and he wished he had chosen the green for his night's lodging, after all.

At that moment a door on his right opened, and a stout, ruddy-faced woman appeared on the threshhold. Her sleeves were rolled to her elbows, and her hands were covered with flour. Instantly her eyes fell on Lance.

"What is it ye'll have, lad?" she asked quickly.

Before Lance could answer, the sad-looking person spoke for him. "He'd like a room for the night, ma'am, but I told him—"

The woman cut him short. "Drag out the cot that's under the eaves." She turned to Lance. " 'Tis no more than the truth we're full up, but if ye don't mind a bit of a corner beneath the very roof itself, sit ye down here till Andrew brings word the cot is made up. 'Tis on the floor ye'd sleep did I lodge ye with these wagoners."

Lance drew a deep sigh of relief. "I do thank you kindly, ma'am," he said earnestly.

Choosing a seat where he could watch whatever went on, he settled down to wait. Gradually, however, the heat of the fire and the stuffy atmosphere of the room made him so drowsy that he was actually nodding and might have gone fast asleep had he not felt a firm hand on his shoulders.

"Where you from, sonny?"

He looked up quickly into a pair of gray eyes which seemed to bore into him like gimlets.

"Where you from, sonny?" The question was repeated.

Lance hesitated, saw that the other noticed his hesitation. But where was he really from, now that his home was ashes?

"Up Valley Mill way," he said finally.

"Valley Mill? Valley Mill? That's beyant Pierce's Corners?"

Lance nodded, and wriggled out from under the hand on his shoulder. There was something about the pressure of that hand he didn't like.

"If I have my bearin's kerrect, Valley Mills is not so far from that there Myst'ry Holler there's so much talk about. You ever been near that Holler, sonny?"

Temptation was strong on Lance to say no, but something his father once said popped into his mind. "Telling a lie is more than wrong. It's silly. It's likely to get you into a heap more trouble than the truth would have kept you out of."

So, "Yes," he said briefly, "I have."

"And where you headed for now?" persisted the other. "Better come clean, sonny, or else—"

But Lance was beginning to resent what seemed to him too many unwarranted inquiries into his personal affairs by a stranger. He rose to his feet, and was glad to see coming toward him at that very moment the sad-faced person the woman had spoken of as Andrew.

"Is my bed ready?" he asked hopefully.

"If by bed you mean that fallin'-apart cot," said Andrew mournfully, "which I just drug out from under the eaves, I 'spose it is. Ye'll find it by climbin' a ladder through yonder trap door into the loft. And it's two bits ye have to pay, she says."

Lance put his hand into his pocket, and brought out a handful of coins from which he took a single piece of silver, noticing as he did so that his questioner of a moment ago had stepped nearer to watch the transaction. "Show me where that ladder is," he told Andrew. "I'm going to bed right now."

The cot, in spite of the lugubrious Andrew's description, proved comfortable enough and the heavy trap door in the attic floor kept out most of the noise from below. Lance's last waking thought was, "This *is* better than spending the night on the green!"

He had been asleep for several hours when something woke him so completely that he sat straight up on the cot, alert and curious. Immediately he felt, rather than saw, for the attic was without a glimmer of light, that someone was lifting the heavy trap door which lay a few feet away from him. Instinctively, he lay down again, ducking under the blanket so as to appear asleep. His heart was pounding as he was sure it had never pounded before.

The next instant a hand holding a squat, lighted candle was thrust through the opening, followed by the head of the man with gray, gimlet eyes. Setting his candle on the floor, he wormed his body through the trap door, then picked up the candle and stood, bent-shouldered because of the low-peaked roof, and looked about him.

Lance, staring out between folds of the blanket, saw in the flickering candlelight his unwelcome visitor pick up his breeches from the floor where he had dropped them and thrust his hand into first one pocket, and then the other. "Just a plain, ornery thief," reflected Lance, "and there goes the money for my journey cakes!"

For a moment the man turned his back to the cot; then Lance heard the breeches fall to the floor, and presently, candle, loot, and all, the intruder descended through the trap door.

All desire to sleep had left Lance for the time being. Not that he was overmuch worried at the prospect of making his way back to Valley Mill without food. He had often been hungry since the death of his father. Nor were there any disturbing noises to prevent slumber. Once the rumble of wagon wheels and the clot-clot of horses' hoofs on the dirt road indicated a wagoner making an early start for some distant destination. Once the yap-yapping of a fox tricked him into believing for an instant that he was back in the clearing on the rim of the

Hollow, whose mystery seemed known even here in Rutland Village so many miles away. But for the most part the deep quiet of night enveloped him.

No, what kept him awake was a troubling premonition that he had not seen the last of the man with the gray, gimlet eyes. Was he really just the plain, "ornery thief" Lance thought him? or was he something more—something which tied him up with the mystery of the Hollow, mention of which he had made the night before?

At last, however, he fell asleep, and when he woke again a pale light was seeping through the cracks in the slanting roof.

"I'm going to leave right away," he decided. "It's no use to wait for any journey cakes, seeing I have no money with which to pay for them."

It was chilly once he had crawled from under the blankets, and he dressed hurriedly, anxious now to be gone before anyone was astir. Quietly raising the trap door, he climbed down the ladder to the room below.

The long logs in the fireplace smouldered under their banking of ashes. In front of them, head pillowed on his great coat, sprawled a snoring wagoner who had arrived too late to secure even a third of a bed. Empty mugs and flagons stood about on the tables, and the air of the room was disagreeably musty and stale. A hound dog, curled beneath a bench, lifted his head and thumped his tail on the floor, but, to Lance's intense relief, did not bark.

Tiptoeing to the door and lifting the great bar that

held it shut, he stepped over the threshhold, closing the door behind him.

Drawing a long, deep breath of the cold, sweet, pine-scented air, he stood for a moment looking about him. Across the green, he could see the little house where he would have spent the night had not Dilsie Buell gone to Hazen Notch to housekeep for her brother. At both his left and his right, mountains lifted against the sky, those in the east bathed in the rosy light of dawn. It was a beautiful morning. Just the sort of a morning a fellow would pick to start on a forty-mile walk, with or without a penny in his pocket or a bite to eat.

But it was too chilly to stand still, and Lance started on a dog trot down the road, thrusting, as he did so, both hands into his breeches pockets.

The next instant he was standing stock still again. Had that strange episode of the night before, the rummaging in his pockets by the man with the gray, gimlet eyes, been only a dream?

It must have been, he thought in bewilderment, as he withdrew a hand from the right hand pocket to stare at a palm full of coins. Yet perhaps it hadn't been a dream. Perhaps the man, disgusted at such trifling pickings, had refused to bother with it.

Suddenly Lance's heart skipped a beat. It hadn't been a dream. Nor had the man been too disgusted to play the thief. The big, round copper coin with the rising sun and the stars and the mountains, the coin he had found imbedded in the mud in Mystery Hollow was missing.

Chapter X

" 'West of the Mountains Green—' "

THREE hours later Lance was plodding along the dusty road over which the day before two pairs of horses had borne him with what now seemed incredible speed. Except for two very sour apples he had picked in an orchard beside a deserted cabin, he had had nothing to eat since the bread and tea given him the night before by Dilsie Buell's neighbor. Doubtless his thoughts as he walked would have been fixed entirely on the emptiness of his stomach had they not dwelt even more on the aching of his feet. For Lance was finding out that it was one thing to tramp at leisure the spongy, cushioned floor of the Hollow, and quite another to cover mile after mile on a rough, rutted road.

Three times already he had stopped beside the road to draw off his heavy boots and plunge his feet into the cool waters of Otter Creek. Doing this had, however, cost him at least one chance, possibly two, for a ride.

The first time, a farmer with an empty cart had rumbled past without seeing him at all as he sat on the bank partly screened by alder bushes. The second time, the driver of a rattletrap sort of vehicle had nearly fallen from his seat to give Lance an elaborate salute with a gay, beribboned whip, but had not slowed down.

The rattletrap vehicle had hardly disappeared in its

97

cloud of dust when Lance remembered he had seen the driver before. He was no other than the queer person who had spoken to him last night on the green, and had called him "tavern company." Tavern company indeed! Lance smiled wryly as he worked his puffy, reddened toes back into their shoes. Tavern company did not travel on foot.

Yet it was at a tavern that Lance hoped to buy what would have to serve as breakfast, dinner, and probably supper. He remembered that the stage had stopped at Pierce's Corner to pick up a mail sack at a vine-covered building with a long, broad ell, and that a sign had swung in front of it, lettered "Bowman Tavern." Surely the few coins he had in his pocket would buy food enough to take the edge from that prodigious appetite which was increasing every minute.

He was beginning to wonder if he had only imagined that tavern, when, rounding a curve in the road, he came upon it exactly as he remembered it. It stood where the highway branched, one fork going, as the rough wooden signboards announced, to "Ye Towne of Brattleborough," and the other, to "Ye Towne of Bennington." A banner of smoke waved from the inn's chimney and several teams stood in the doorway.

Hungry though he was, Lance hesitated. Should he go in through the main entrance, or should he knock at the door of the ell? As he waited to make up his mind, he saw on the other side of the road, just beyond the tavern, the rattletrap vehicle which had passed him as he sat on the bank of Otter Creek. The white horse which drew it, a creature as bony and gaunt as its master, was feeding with nose buried deep in a nosebag. The driver was nowhere to be seen.

I wish I knew which road he's taking, thought Lance. When I come out, I'll ask him.

A second later the door of the ell was opened to his knock by a plump little man with a pancake turner in his hand, and in no time at all Lance faced a platter of flapjacks smothered in maple syrup. When he came out again both his appetite and the flapjacks had disappeared. So, too, had the bony horse and his rattletrap wagon.

Lance, after a brief pang of disappointment, turned resolutely to the left along the Brattleborough Pike, aware that when he reached the farther side of the mountain whose summit loomed ahead, he would have completed about half of his journey. At the foot of that slope nestled a hamlet and there he must see what arrangements he could make for the night. An offer to grain and rub down the horses or milk the cow should be worth at least a bed in the haymow, he figured.

His way for the present lay along the valley of a stream which emptied into Otter Creek. Its noisy rush over the stony bottom could be heard through the trees and underbrush beside the road. Now and then a break in the forest, where lumbering had been carried on, afforded a vista of sunlit meadows and distant mountain ranges. For the most part, however, he was shut in by a leafy wall of evergreens mixed with sugar maples, aspen, and birch.

In spite of the fact that he was no longer hungry and that his feet were troubling him less than they had on the other, more deeply rutted road, Lance's spirits were low. He dreaded the prospect of reporting to M'ma Chapelle that the journey had been fruitless, that the money used for it from her slender savings had been wasted. Moreover, his own fate seemed inevitably linked with that of "those Chapelles." How could he abandon them to face the winter alone? Yet how could he stay with them and find time to solve the mystery of the Hollow? When that was accomplished, would he be able to get a job in the iron works at Bennington and start earning money with which to buy a horse of his very own?

Just one thing—and one alone—could happen to solve his problem, and that was the return of P'pa Chapelle. But it was a solution in which Lance no longer had any faith. If P'pa Chapelle had been coming back, he would have come long ago. If he had not been coming back, or had been delayed, he would have written. He had not come back. He had not written. Therefore, reasoned Lance, P'pa Chapelle must be dead, and he, Lance, had inherited a ready-made family, entailing responsibilities he didn't in the least want to assume. Every step he took along this winding, shaded road was bringing him nearer those responsibilities.

He was beginning to feel the pull of the grade that would eventually take him over the mountain, when he heard the sound of a human voice coming from a point just beyond the next bend in the road. He stood still to listen. There was a peculiar carrying power in its nasal twang.

"Fare ye well, ma'am! Fare ye well! Look for me again come spring! Git a move on, old Bag o' bones! I'll make it a point, ma'am, to tote along that red kaliker fer yer kitchen winder curtain. D'ye think I feed ye so ye'll freeze in yer tracks? 'Twill look right smart, ma'am, in that winder.

'West o' the Mountains Green lies Rutland fair—' "

Lance broke into a run and reached the bend just in time to see the head and shoulders of an old white horse push through the leafy fringes of a lane that doubtless led to a clearing on the river. Lance had recognized that nasal voice, and this time was determined that the owner of it should not get away from him.

"Hi!" he yelled at the top of his lungs. "Hi!"

" 'The best that e'er was seen for soil and air;
   Oh, west o' the Mountains Green lies—"

went on the voice.

"Hi!" yelled Lance again, as the rattletrap of a wagon emerged into full view, and he could see its driver waving his whip in time to the song. "Hi!"

The song stopped abruptly. So did the horse and wagon at a sudden jerk of the reins.

"So-o-o— If it ain't Mr. Tavern Company in person! I'm completely kerflummexed!"

"Please don't call me that any more!" exclaimed Lance impatiently. "I—are you going toward Valley Mill?"

The other cocked his head, which still had on it partly over one ear the scrap of hat with a red feather, and seemed to be meditating on Lance's question with great gravity. Finally, "I'm a-goin' to Brattleborough," he declared, "and I'm a-goin' there one o' two ways. I'm either a-flyin' from peak to peak on a witch's broomstick, or else I'm a-stayin' right on this pike which passes straight through that little town you mention. Could it be ye'd like to j'ine me on my little throne?"

As a matter of fact, Lance was now of two minds. Did he, or did he not, want to travel with this queer person? A twinge in his aching feet decided him. "I'd like to very much," he said quickly.

The driver stretched down a hand and helped Lance over the wheel. "There ye be!" he said amiably. "Step lively, Bag o' bones."

The next instant Lance nearly fell from his high perch, as his companion, picking up his song on the very note he had broken off, let out a sudden bellow. " '—Rutland *fair*, the *best* that e'er was *seen* for soil and *air*.' " He turned to Lance. "T'other side o' the mountain, I've an excellent one about 'Fort Dummer was named for Sir William, tra la!' "

He paused, and Lance felt that he was expected to say something. "Are you a—a traveling musician, sir?" he asked politely.

"Me? Musician? Take a squint inside my wagon, lad. 'Twill tell ye my name 'n occerpation."

Lance twisted about on the seat and stared into the vehicle's interior. Every square inch of space was crammed with pots and pans and kettles of every description, some of tin, some of copper, many of iron. Those of tin and copper were polished until they shone like the morning sun.

"So now ye know. I'm Tin Peddler Joe," rhymed the man beside him. "Ever hear tell o' me?"

Lance nodded. He had heard M'ma Chapelle complain more than once, "Buried in the wilderness we are. Why, even Tin Peddler Joe never gets to come where we live!" He felt much easier in his mind. Tin Peddler Joe might be odd and look something like a scarecrow, but he was harmless enough; and what a piece of luck it was to pick up this ride with him!

"Time that there Pierre Chapelle came back from wherever he's at. Iffen the winter should tighten up early same's I've seen it do many a year, his wife 'n young uns could be snowbound in their four walls till the spring thaw. Have to live on their own fat!"

"You—you know those Chapelles?" asked Lance in surprise.

"Know of 'em. I get me around. And them I pick up generally lets fall bits about folks."

An interesting idea occurred to Lance. Perhaps the peddler, in the course of his journeying, had at some time run across the one-armed man. He decided, when a suitable opportunity arose, to question him, but in such a casual way that no suspicion would be roused in the other's mind of undue concern on his part.

In the meantime he could not resist making an experiment.

"You—you wouldn't know a man in Rutland Village with—with gray eyes—" he began.

The peddler shoved his scrap of hat still further over his ear and scratched his head. "Rutland Village—man with gray eyes—pretty tall, is he?"

"Yes," said Lance. "Tall, and—well, he had a way of looking right through you—"

"Oh, him!" The other shrugged his shoulders. "Sure I know him. Sold his wife an iron kettle only yesterday ter cook apple mash fer the pigs in. He hangs around Mead's Inn. Part of his job to keep an eye on strangers 'n vagrants comin' ter town."

"Oh," said Lance faintly.

"He's town constable. Mighty nice fellow iffen ye keep inside the law. Iffen ye don't, he's a wicked one." He lifted his whip from its socket and once more broke into song.

> " 'We *value* not New *York,*
> With *all* their *powers.*
> For *here* we'll *stay* and *work.*
> The *land* is *ours.*' "

But Lance was not listening. So the man who had climbed up through the trap door and had taken the copper coin from his breeches pocket had not been the thief he thought him. On the contrary, perhaps the constable regarded *him* as a thief. He remembered how he had felt the man's eyes watching him as he took out his money to pay Andrew for the night's lodging. He must have seen the copper coin then. But what was there about that coin which made it different from any other! Perhaps it wasn't copper at all. Perhaps it was really gold. Perhaps it had originally been stolen by the man who had dropped it in the Hollow.

Lance drew a deep breath. He was glad indeed to be leaving Rutland Village behind him. Glad he had risen early and left the tavern before anyone was up. Suppose the constable had planned to arrest him and clap him into the little stone jail—

Tin Peddler Joe was flourishing his whip, wagging his head, and singing at the top of his voice.

> " 'West of the Mountains *Green*
> Lies Rutland fair;
> The best that e'er was *seen*
> For soil and air!' "

But Lance didn't even hear him.

Chapter XI

"He's an out 'n out bad 'un!"

"T̲ER my mind there's nothing like a coupla wide-awake fried eggs 'n a slab o' bacon washed down with a pot o' hot tea ter start the day off prancin'. Help yerself, Tavern Company."

Bright morning sunshine was filtering through the pines and even driving the dark shadows from Clarendon Gorge, which lay across the river from the point where Tin Peddler Joe and Lance had spent the night. Blue smoke rose straight heavenward from the fire where, held in place by an iron tripod, a smoke-blackened skillet sizzled and sputtered with enough food, thought Lance, to keep him alive for a month.

"I suppose," he said with a sigh, "you never will call me anything but that."

"What's that? What's that? Oh, yes, ter be sure. Ter be sure. Well, now, 'tis like old Bag o' bones here!" He slapped affectionately the thin flank of the white horse who stood sociably near, cropping the sparse grass growing among the pine needles. "Her real name is Cora. Former owner told me so. But when I first lay eyes on her she didn't look a mite like Cora to me. She looked like a bag o' bones, 'n has ever since, no matter how I cossett her. So Bag o' bones she is to me, not meanin' offense ter her *or* you. When I spoke ter ye last evenin' on Rutland

Village green, thinkin' yer might be a stranger in need o' lodgin' I could provide, ye spoke up so quick 'n proud-like, 'I'm a-stayin' at Mead's Inn', why, you was tavern company from then on ter me. That's how I am!"

Lance couldn't help laughing at the other's earnest explanation. Then he sobered, remembering ruefully the jouncings of the day before yesterday and what had happened to his copper coin. "I like this very much better than stagecoach and tavern travel," he said emphatically.

Several stops had been made the afternoon before in the tiny hamlet on the eastern slope of the mountain. The peddler patted the heads of the children who swarmed in and out of his wagon, admired the geraniums and sampled the jams of their mothers, and at no place sold less than half-a-dozen articles and took orders "on my next trip come spring" for no fewer than half-a-dozen more.

Dusk had fallen when, leaving the highway, he drove into a level grove extending to the river which here brawled over a series of rapids.

" 'Tis a regular campin' ground o' mine," he had told Lance. "Under twenty layers o' needles, ye'd find the ashes o' my first fire when I started tin peddlin' that number o' years ago after my discharge from Ira Allen's Herrick's Rangers."

Lance had looked about him. "All those needles ought to make a pretty comfortable bed," he said.

"We ain't a-sleepin' on any pine needles," retorted the peddler. "I may not be tavern company, but I'm one who likes his bed comfortable. We're a-sleepin' in the wagon."

"Both of us?" asked Lance, turning to look again at the wagon's crowded insides. "I don't mind sleeping on the ground. I've done it very often. I don't mind it at all." Secretly he was thinking he'd just about as soon sleep in the river as in that jumbled mess of pots and pans.

"Both o' us, lad. And snug as two black-eyed beans in a pod."

And so it had proved. With Lance's help the peddler removed his stock, nesting those kettles which could be nested, and turning the rest upside down under a tarpaulin. When the bottom of the wagon was cleared, Lance saw that it was divided into two halves which lifted on hinges and fastened back against the sides, disclosing a bed already made up with blankets and quilts and two goosefeather pillows.

" 'Tis no invention o' mine," disclaimed Tin Peddler Joe modestly. "In fact, 'tis a device used commonly ter transport bondsmen from Alabamy way over the border ter Canady."

"I don't suppose—" began Lance, and then stopped short. That was hardly the sort of thing one could ask about.

But the peddler seemed to know what was in Lance's mind. "No," he said. "I never have."

Within ten minutes of the time Lance had taken off his boots and climbed over the tailboard into the bed, which rested easily on the springs beneath, he was sound asleep. When his eyes opened again, the sun was shining, two squirrels were scolding on a limb above the wagon top, and the air was fragrant with the blended odors of pine trees, wood smoke, and frying bacon.

"Fort Dummer was named for Sir William, tra la!
Fort Dummer was named for he—"

No sooner was breakfast over, and Tin Peddler Joe had climbed to his seat, helped Lance over the wheel, and snatched his whip from its socket, than he burst into song, which seemed this time, to consist of just two lines repeated over and over.

Lance waited until the peddler was forced to pause for breath, then he put a question to him. "Do you make up your own songs?"

"I made up that 'un," admitted his companion. "But not the one you heerd yesterday. 'West o' the Mountains Green—' Not that 'un. 'Twas writ by Thomas Rowley, one o' Ethan Allen's men. Come from Danby. Just beyant Pierce Corner a ways on the Bennington Pike. But I don't sing 'West o' the Mountains Green' this side the divide. From now on, it's 'Fort Dummer was named for Sir William.' "

"But if you've only made up two lines—"

"That's right, Tavern Company," said Tin Peddler Joe sadly. "Two lines—that's all I ever got ter make up."

Their way lay through a sparsely settled region covered with long unbroken stretches of heavy timber. Twice a deer made a graceful loop in front of them from thicket to thicket, and once a mother skunk led five little ones almost under the very hoofs of the horse. The road followed the river, but for the most part the stream could only be heard, not seen.

As the morning passed and they drew nearer to Valley Mill, Lance grew steadily more unhappy. Finally, in an effort to put the Chapelles out of his mind and especially the picture of M'ma Chapelle's face as it would be when he told her his discouraging news, he strove to think only about his own plans. He tried to think how, if he were free to do as he liked, he would carry them out. And suddenly he decided to sound out his companion on the subject of the one-armed man.

"Mr.—," he began, but stopped, realizing for the first time that he did not know the other's last name.

"No 'mister', thank ye kindly. Just plain 'Tin Peddler Joe'," the peddler helped him out.

"Well, then, Tin Peddler Joe, you—you must meet a lot of persons in your travels, and you did know right away who the man with the gray eyes in Mead's Inn was. Did you ever, that is—well, did you ever come across a man with one arm?"

"A man with one arm—" repeated the peddler, shoving his scrap of cap with its little red feather farther down one ear and scratching his head, a gesture now grown familiar to Lance whenever his companion wanted to think.

"Ter be sure, Tavern Company, ter be sure I know a man with one arm. Step lively there, Bag o' bones. This ain't the up-grade on the Camel's Hump. Lost it in the battle o' Hubbarton. Anybody'd think ye had no sperrit, walking on the level. Lives up ter Gookins' Falls. Sold his wife a feed bucket. Goes by the name—"

"But—"

"—o' Hickok. Raises sheep and swine, he does. Like-wise—"

"But—"

"—draught horses. All o' six feet two he be. Kin lift a corn crib clear o' the ground with his one good arm. Never wears a hat. Hair's bleached the color o' sand. Sold his sister—"

"But that's not the man I'm talking about, Tin Ped-dler Joe. The one I mean is short and wears a round cap of weasel fur."

The peddler shoved his scrap of a hat back on his ear again. "Round cap o' weasel fur? Heck, why in all git-out didn't ye say so first-off? Ter be sure I know him. He's an out 'n out bad 'un. Likewise ye wrong 'bout his havin' only one arm. I've a-seen him when he 'peared ter have only one leg. Fact is, he's got two arms, two legs, two eyes, and an evil heart 'n I'm a-handin' ye this advice. Iffen ever he comes nigh, put a range o' high mountains 'twixt you 'n him, quicker 'n scat."

"Is—is the law after him?"

"The law's allus arter him 'n his gang. They be forced ter move from one hideout ter another, keepin' jest one lap ahead o' gettin' caught."

"But what is it they're up to?"

Tin Peddler Joe opened his mouth, shut it again, shrugged his shoulders. Lance saw it would do no good to question him further. He was almost sorry he had questioned him at all. What had he learned that he didn't know already?

Certainly it was no news to him that the man was evil. That fact was written all over his sinister face. Nor was he surprised that the law was trailing him and his companions. Lance had long suspected that whatever was being carried on in the Hollow was illegal. As for finding out that the fellow's lack of an arm had been mere pretense—the peddler's words had simply confirmed what Lance had seen with his own eyes when the men passed him on the trail the day he was overtaken in the Hollow by the storm.

The advice to put a mountain range between him and the man in the weasel-fur cap was as completely lost as dandelion fluff on a summer wind as he vowed to himself, "Chapelles or no Chapelles, I won't let up on that Hollow!"

He and Tin Peddler Joe parted in front of the Fish and Turtle, Lance to pick up Wash and Jeff at Farmer Bob Evans', his host of the past twenty-four hours to show his wares to the women of Valley Mill.

The peddler's last words to him were a promise. "Soon as ever I get the chance, I'll call on them Chapelles. Tell 'em from me how some day they'll hark to a rattle 'n bang, 'n there'll be Tin Peddler Joe a-drivin' old Bag o' bones inter their very dooryard." With a spectacular flourish of his whip, he swung down the lane that led to the home of the whitesmith, and a moment later, even above the roll of wagon wheels, Lance could hear,

"Fort Dummer is named for Sir William, tra la!
    Fort Dummer is named for he—"

Lance made his way soberly over the covered bridge, reluctant to start on the long, slow ride back to the Chapelle farm. Bag o' bones was no little Figure, as he remembered Farmer Evans had called his little stallion, but she was a race horse when compared with Wash and Jeff. Also he knew he was bound to miss the lively chatter and sudden outbursts of song of Tin Peddler Joe who, now that Lance was better acquainted with him, no longer seemed queer. And the thought of what awaited him at the end of the journey was no inducement to hurry.

He had almost reached the Evans home when he saw a light cart rolling down the road toward him. It was drawn by—yes, it was actually the little bay, with Farmer Evans driving.

Lance broke into a run, reaching the cart just as the farmer recognized him and called out a "Whoa," which the bay instantly obeyed. "Been expectin 'ye," said Farmer Evans genially. "The team's hitched and ready. Journey successful?"

"Not very," admitted Lance, gently stroking Figure's smooth, silk neck.

The farmer waited a moment, but Lance, not sure that

M'ma Chapelle would want him to discuss her affairs, said nothing further, and Farmer Evans picked up his reins. "I'm on my way to make arrangements fer Fair Day. Better plan to get down if ye can. Big doin's."

"I'd like to see it," said Lance. He had heard the Chapelles talk about Fair Day. "But I reckon I'll be tied up for a spell."

"Well—good luck to ye!" Farmer Evans gave a "Clk", and he and the bay were away in a cloud of dust.

Lance, staring after them, drew a long, deep sigh. Lucky Farmer Evans just to be driving that little horse!

Chapter XII

"There's something I must find out—"

DARKNESS, brought on by the approach of a storm, as well as by the night, had fallen several hours before Lance reached the farm. He had, in fact, hardly left Valley Mill behind him before he noticed that the sun, which had shone so brightly that very morning in the pine grove opposite Clarendon Gorge, was now sinking toward a gray bank of cloud well above the horizon. The wind had risen and although he did not feel it, riding mostly in the shelter of thick woods, he could hear it moving above him in the treetops.

It's getting awfully cold, he thought suddenly, and hugged the heavy horse blanket closer around him. At the same moment he felt something wet and stinging on his cheek. And then another. And a third.

Snow! He hadn't figured on snow so soon. What was it Tin Peddler Joe had said about winter tightening down early? Snow in any great amount would serously affect his plans about the Hollow, for snow, whether one went afoot or on snowshoes, left tracks. The flakes continued to fall lazily, steadily.

By the time he reached the farm everything was white.

The Chapelles were waiting for him. No sooner had the heavy wheels of the wagon crunched over the frozen ruts into the drive than the door flew open and Mathilde burst out, holding up a lighted lantern and at the same time struggling into her father's greatcoat.

"I'll—I'll help you unhitch!" she cried. Her teeth were chattering, but whether from cold or excitement at his return, Lance did not know.

He climbed down slowly, stiffly. If only somebody else were in his shoes and he were anywhere else but here!

For a moment he was tempted to tell Mathilde of the journey's failure, but decided against it. To do so would mean performing a disagreeable task twice. Taking the lantern, he led the oxen into the shelter of the barn and, with Mathilde's for-once eager assistance, unyoked them. Dreading the time when he must go into the house, he was so deliberate in hanging up the pieces of harness on their proper pegs and in throwing down the hay from the mow into the stalls that Mathilde became impatient and stamped her foot. "You *are* such a slowpoke!" she scolded.

"I'm all through," he said at last. "Is—is your mother any stronger than when I left?"

"I don't know. Maybe. But she'll be all right just as soon as we get to Cousin Dilsie's. She's been packing all day."

So M'ma Chapelle had been "packing all day." She'd be all right just as soon as she got to Cousin Dilsie's. Lance felt that he'd rather turn and run blindly into the storm than enter the house.

As it happened, Lance didn't actually have to tell his story even once. As he stepped slowly over the threshhold into the warm, firelit kitchen, M'ma Chapelle hurried toward him, both hands held out. Then her arms dropped to her sides, and she sat down quickly in a chair beside the table. But she didn't take her eyes from his face.

"You—you didn't bring me any letter from Pierre," she said heavily. "Cousin Dilsie can't take us in. I can tell from the very way you look. Perhaps she doesn't want us."

"It isn't like that!" exclaimed Lance. "It isn't like that at all." Now that the worst was known, he was eager to soften the blow, even by a little. "She's gone to Hazen Notch to housekeep for her brother. She'd even left before I got there. A neighbor woman told me, and said some family from up Middleb'ry way is going to move in."

"I should have known something like that would happen," said M'ma Chapelle wearily. She continued to sit so still, looking so long into the fire, that Mathilde went over and stood beside her.

Suddenly, and to his own great surprise, Lance heard

himself announcing a decision quite as if he were in the habit of announcing decisions on the spur of the moment. Not only that. He was uttering it as calmly and matter-of-factly as if it were something he didn't mind doing. "If you would like to have me, Mrs. Chapelle," he said, "I'll stay here and help you run the farm until your husband comes back, no matter how long it is."

For a moment M'ma Chapelle didn't say a word. Then she spoke very kindly. "That's right good of you, Lance. 'Tain't reasonable you should, though. You've got your own life to live, and I know you've a hankerin' for a regular man's job in the iron works. Then, too, there's no tellin' about Pierre. 'Tis true he's a rover. Allus thinkin' it's better beyond the next range o' hills. But he's not one to abandon his family. It's just that something—something must have happened to him."

At that moment a great gust of wind shook the little house. M'ma Chapelle shivered. "And you'd better leave right away. Once we're snowed in, 'twill be for keeps, here in the mountains the way we be."

Lance had to fight a strong temptation to agree that she was right, that he should go, and go soon, without waiting even long enough to clear up that mystery in the Hollow. Suppose P'pa Chapelle were really dead, and there was plenty of reason to suppose he must be, not coming back before this and not even answering M'ma Chapelle's letters—

"I'm staying," he said stoutly, "and I'm hungry."

Hill slopes and meadows and the roofs of barn and

lean-to were glistening white with snow when Lance went out to milk the cow and feed and water all the animals the next morning. But the wind no longer howled, and the outside ledge of the south window inside of which M'ma Chapelle grew her pots of lavender and marjoram was dripping in the warm sun.

Cherry whinnied at sight of him, and Lance tried to think the little colt was glad to see him, and not just the measure of oats he carried. He cleaned out the stall, brought fresh bedding, lingered to stroke the chestnut's glossy flanks. "If you could go as fast as Figure," he said, "I could like you as much as I do him. You really are every bit as handsome!"

Back in the kitchen, he sat down to the dish of yellow corn mush 'Tilda had ladled from the iron kettle which had hung all night over the warm ashes on the hearth. Milk which he himself had brought in and a spoonful of maple sap made it taste as good as the flapjacks had tasted at Bowman's Tavern, or even Tin Peddler Joe's wide awake eggs.

But Lance's thoughts did not linger on his food. He was planning his course of action on the night, now so near at hand, when the moon would be full. And he kept right on planning it, in spite of the twins' noisy tussle with Boney, the clatter of Mathilde's stacking dishes, even the questions M'ma Chapelle just couldn't seem to help asking. "Were there many stores in Rutland Village?" "Did folks seem friendly like?" "What did you say the woman on the stage was wearing, the one with the little boy?"

Lance answered her, could hear himself answering her; yet all the time his mind was on the mystery of the Hollow, and how, without letting anyone know, especially prying Mathilde, he was going to solve it.

His days resumed a familiar pattern. There was always the stock to be cared for, water to be brought from the well into the house, wood to be chopped, and odd jobs that varied with the day and the weather.

His one delight was Cherry, his one recreation a ride down the road or over the fields and up the slope of the hill where the little chestnut had once stumbled into a chuck hole. Lance kept his eyes wide open for more such chuck holes, and Cherry herself seemed to have developed an instinct for side-stepping them.

It was on returning from one such excursion, taken late in the afternoon, that he brought Cherry to a halt on a small knoll half way back to the farm house. Lying dark against the glow of a bright sunset, was the Ridge, on the other side of which lay the heart of the Hollow. It seemed to him, seated on Cherry and staring across valley and hills, very, very far away. As for the spot on the Ox Road where the trail into the Hollow started and where he planned to lie in wait for the man with the weasel-fur cap and his friends—that too, although much nearer than the Ridge, was all of several miles from where he was now.

How was he going to steal away, complete his task of stalking the men, once they had appeared, and retrace the distance back to the farm without telling M'ma Chapelle his plans? Yet, if he did not tell her, he would cause her a great deal of alarm over his unexplained absence.

The obvious thing to do—so it seemed to him—slipped into Lance's mind, and he remembered his previous intention.

"Cherry, I'm going to ride you!" He heard himself say the words aloud. "We'll just leave quietly, you and I, when everyone's asleep—and when everyone wakes up, we'll be back home again. I'll hide you in the forest off the trail while I wait, and—and, oh, why didn't I think of this before!"

That same night Lance watched impatiently for the rising moon, and when it finally appeared above the leafless maples, round and yellow and shining and not unlike his lost copper coin, he noted with satisfaction that in three more nights at the most it would be quite full. He realized that there was always the chance that the men might make their journey just before or just after the night when the moon was full, but that was a chance he must take. Also, now that he intended to use Cherry, he resolved to try again on the next night and even the next, should the men not appear in the meanwhile.

The time passed slowly, and when at last the day came on which he planned to go, Lance made his preparations carefully.

First of all, he saw to it that, in case anything did happen to delay him, there was an extra supply of wood at hand, and even a second bucket of water in the kitchen. Mathilde did not fail to observe his forethought.

"You certainly do act as if you thought there was a ten foot blizzard coming," she declared suspiciously, "or as if you figured to be laid low with the smallpox. In all the time you've been staying here, you've never done this before!"

Lance pretended not to hear her, and he was really too much annoyed to answer her politely. She could so easily decide he was up to something, and once she did that, wild horses wouldn't be able to stop her from ferreting out his secret!

Consequently, he took pains to wait until she had taken the twins out for a romp before stuffing several apples into the pockets of his jacket against a possible long and hungry stay in the forest. Later, when she had gone to bed, he stole out to the lean-to and hung the jacket on a convenient peg beside Cherry's saddle.

Finally, he wrote a short note to M'ma Chapelle and left it on an overturned feed bucket in Cherry's stall. She would find it almost as quickly as she would learn of the colt's absence.

"Dear Mrs. Chapelle:

I don't expect you'll ever read this but I figure it wouldn't be fair to leave without saying where I'm going in case something happens so I don't get back as soon as I've planned, especially as I'm riding Cherry. It's like this. There's something I must find out, and I can only do it by visiting the edge of the Hollow tonight. Don't worry, even if I am later getting back than I mean to be. I'll be very careful of Cherry.

Lance.

P.S. 'Tilda can milk if she has to."

Lance went to bed with all his clothes on, his shoes on the floor within easy reach. The moon would not rise until nearly midnight and by then he expected to be well on his way. But first he must be sure that no one else was awake.

The twins, as he had known they would be, were asleep almost as soon as they pulled the blankets over them. Mathilde was next. Through the thin partition he could hear her deep, untroubled breathing. But it seemed as though M'ma Chapelle would never stop turning and twisting. Just as he thought she had fallen asleep, the twisting and turning would begin all over again.

At length, however, she had lain still for so long Lance decided it was safe to attempt his getaway.

Shoes in his hand, he tiptoed toward the outer door. Boney, lying on the warm hearth, lifted his head, but dropped it again, and the next moment Lance was outside and noticing with a frown that already a silver light showed in the east. He was not leaving a minute too soon.

Chapter XIII

"Don't make a sound!"

LANCE, riding Cherry through the night, felt as if he were moving on wings. The last time he had traveled along this road had been the evening of the day when he had found his cabin a smoking ruin. Now one landmark after another slipped by and, suddenly there he was at the fork. There one branch led to the left to the clearing, and the other to the right, to the spot he was seeking, the point where the trail to the Hollow began.

He took the latter, and soon afterward slowed Cherry to a walk, afraid he would pass the inconspicuous entrance to the trail without noticing it. As a matter of fact, he was already wondering if he had passed it and should turn back, when, in the moonlight sifting through the trees, he saw a few marks at the side of the road which might indicate the approach to some path into the underbrush.

Dismounting, but keeping fast hold of the bridle lest Cherry should bolt, he examined the bushes for several feet until he found a place where they were broken as if someone had made his way through them. Yes, there was no mistake about it. This was the point where the trail from the Hollow met the road. Here was the spot where he must wait.

The next step was to hide Cherry, and he walked down the road several yards from the trail, seeking a suitable cover. When he found one and sought to lead the little horse to it, Cherry did not take kindly to the plan. On the contrary, she braced her front feet, tossed her head, and snorted angrily.

"Please, Cherry," wheedled Lance, "I'll come back for you. Do please stay here and *keep quiet!*" By dint of tugging and coaxing, he finally managed to get her near enough to the lower limb of a maple tree to fasten her so securely she could not break loose.

"I hope she doesn't thrash around or whinny," worried Lance.

Leaving Cherry with one last apologetic pat on her silky, wilful nose, Lance returned to the trail to take up a position where he could hear, and even see, whatever went on in the trail. By luck he found a fallen spruce so great of girth that he could crouch behind it and peer over the top, perfectly camouflaged in the background of trees, even with the moonlight at its brightest. There was nothing to do now but wait.

Making himself as comfortable as possible, he wondered if he had been right in not bringing along old Eagle-eye, and decided that he had. Tonight he had no intention of putting himself in a position where he might have to defend himself. That time would almost surely come later, he suspected. For the present he was being the stalker, the spy, and the less encumbered he was, the better.

Slowly the moon rose higher and higher above the trees, her silver light flooding the portion of the trail on which he kept his eyes glued. If they're going to come at all, they must come soon, he found himself thinking, and at the thought little shivers played a game of tag up and down his spine.

But the minutes passed, and nothing happened. Once Lance was certain he heard something moving in the brush behind him, and his heart somersaulted in his breast. The something proved only a slender doe, who bounded lightly over the farther end of the fallen spruce into the trail and was gone. Once, far away toward the Ridge, a fox yapped, and constantly there were all sorts of strange little creature noises very close at hand.

He was not cold, for the weather had turned mild, but after a while he became hungry, and ate two of the apples he had stuffed into his jacket pockets.

When, finally, the men did come, there were three of them, not just two, as he had expected. He heard their voices long before he saw them and judged from the sound that they were quarreling. As they drew nearer, he was able to make out something of what they were saying.

"I'm tellin' ye, 'tis the last o' these danged trips I'll take. 'Twouldn't be so bad iffen we had a pack mule."

"Quittin', be ye? Gittin' lazy, be ye?"

"Mebbe I'm quittin'. Mebbe I ain't. But 'tis time we got clear o' this place. 'Tain't healthy."

"Gittin' afeerd o' yer own shadder, be ye? Or d'ye meanta. . . ." But the rest of the speaker's words Lance could not catch.

"Mebbe I do. Mebbe I don't. But iffen Dawes don't show up some time and the law do, an' we git caught red-handed, it'll mean jail fare for which I don't hanker."

"Shut up, the two o' ye!" It was a third voice, an ugly, snarling voice, and instantly Lance knew it for the voice of the man with the weasel-fur hat and the evil countenance. "It's me that says who'll quit 'n when. Ye both in this up to yer danged necks. Tell Dawes ter be on hand fer the split at Jake's this day week. Tell him—what's that danged noise?"

Faintly, very faintly, a thin, small, unhappy sound drifted through the woods. Lance's blood congealed slowly in his veins. The sound was Cherry whinnying to be set free.

Would it come again?

"Some folks is 'feerd o' a screech owl!" sneered the

man whose voice Lance had heard first. "Me—I'm not 'feerd o' screech owls. Jest 'feerd o' jail fare, I be."

Lance heard two sudden, heavy thuds, as of two heavy burdens thrown to the ground, then a scuffling noise which stopped as quickly as it had begun.

"Ye're both dang fools!" This time it was the voice of the second man he had heard. "Jud here's a fool, 'n ye be un, too, Boss. Moon don't last ferever. Dawes is a-waitin'. Iffen we don't show up, he'll leave, 'n then where'll we be?"

There was no verbal response from the two whom he had evidently separated, but presently, outlined against the trees on the other side of the trail, Lance saw the figure of a man advancing slowly with a heavy sack on his bowed shoulders. Behind him walked a second figure, similarly laden, and behind him a third, but the third carried no load. Silently, doggedly they filed past within a few feet of him, while Lance held his breath and hoped with all his might that the beating of his heart would not betray him, and that Cherry would not whinny again.

His plan was to let them get well-started on the road toward their destination, whatever it was—and from what he had overheard he judged it to be a meeting with one "Dawes"—before he made any effort to leave his hiding place and follow them. It was, he reflected, a moment later, a very lucky thing he had held to his plan.

He was just on the point of climbing over the fallen spruce when he heard the pad of footsteps on the trail, but this time they came from the direction of the road. Was it possible he or Cherry had left prints in the dirt at the entrance to the trail which had been noticed? Had one of the men come back to search him out?

Something told Lance this was unlikely and he was sure of it when a moment later the man with the weasel-fur hat passed along the trail on a dog trot, looking neither to the right nor left.

"I can figure out why he came back," said Lance to himself. "Those bags look to be pretty heavy, whatever is in them. He came along to spell the other two on the trail so's they'd last out the rest of the way. Now he's going back to keep guard at wherever their hiding-place is in the Hollow." He waited, however, until he was sure there was no danger of the man's returning. Then he made his way out to the trail, followed it to the road, and took up his pursuit of the two laden men.

For what seemed several long hours he kept, not at their heels, but, on the contrary, as far in their rear as he could without losing sight of them. He hugged the side of the road, walking with great care lest he give them any reason to suppose themselves shadowed.

As for the distance he must travel before reaching the spot where the men were to meet one "Dawes," he could not believe it was many miles away, yet he had only the vaguest notion as to just where the road they were taking ultimately came out. He knew that it skirted Squaw Hill and sooner or later probably reached the highway somewhere between Valley Mill and Clarendon Gorge opposite which he had camped for the night with Tin Peddler Joe. But one of the speakers had said, "Dawes is waitin'," and that remark seemed to indicate the place of rendezvous must be within a reasonable distance.

As it was, Lance nearly lost his quarry altogether. One moment they were there ahead of him, two plodding figures, plainly visible in the moonlight. The next they had vanished as completely as if the earth had opened up and swallowed them, sacks and all. He started to run. Was there a bend in the road he had not seen? Were his eyes playing tricks on him?

A sudden suspicion that he was rushing into danger halted him just in time, but not before he had reached a gap in the trees on the right hand side of the road and could see a faint wagon trail leading into the woods. That must be where the men had gone, because there was no other place they *could* go.

Without hesitation Lance turned into it. Perhaps the trail was a short cut to the highway. Perhaps it led to a shanty where one "Dawes" was—or was not—still waiting. Perhaps—

"Kep' me waitin' much longer, I'd a left ye flat."

The very nearness of the harsh voice sent Lance's heart into his throat. He slid quickly behind a tree.

Because of the denseness of tall evergreens, the moonlight barely reached the scene at all. Then as Lance's eyes grew used to the dimmer light, he made out a farm wagon backed toward him, filled with sacks similar in appearance to those carried by the two men. On the seat of the wagon sat a figure wrapped in a heavy cloak, and half turned about to speak to the men who had set down their burdens and stood rubbing their backs.

"Hurry 'em into the cart. I be danged sick o' waitin'."

One of the men muttered something which Lance could not catch, but he stopped rubbing his back and reaching into the wagon began lifting out, one at a time, several of the bags with which it was filled. These, Lance could plainly see, by the way the man handled them, resembled the sacks the men had carried, but were not nearly so heavy.

When four or five had been removed, the fellow picked up the sacks he and the other man had brought from the Hollow, put them into the cart, and replaced the bags he had taken out. As he did so, Lance noticed an acrid odor and had trouble stifling a cough as the air about him seemed filled with tiny dustlike particles.

"Pearl ash, that's what's in those bags in the wagon," he said to himself, and remembered how he and his father, when clearing their land, had leached out wood ashes for pearl ashes with which to make soap.

When all the bags were in, the man drew over them a heavy tarpaulin which had been rolled back, and fastened it into place. Then he delivered his message. "Boss says meet at Jake's in Danby this day week."

The figure in the heavy cloak merely grunted, settled back on his seat, spoke to his team, and a moment later figure, team, and wagon had vanished into the darkness of the forest.

As the two men left behind came toward him on the way back to the road, Lance dared not move. Instead, he clung tightly to the tree, hoping to merge his own silhouette with that of the trunk, and the ruse worked for they passed him without so much as a single glance in his direction. Common sense warned him to let them get well started on the return trip before setting out himself, and as he waited he thought with satisfaction of Cherry, standing patiently in the forest covert to carry him the rest of the way home.

Where he left the wagon trail, he broke into a dog trot. Apparently the two men had done the same, for not once did he catch sight of them and when he reached the entrance to the Hollow trail, although he stood stock still a moment to listen, he could hear no sound of either voices or of running feet.

I followed them and I didn't get caught! he thought triumphantly. "And I've learned how they get their stuff out by hiding it in with the pearl ash. Next time I'll stay in the Hollow until I find out just what that stuff is!"

From the entrance to the trail it took him but a minute to reach the place where he had left Cherry. Breaking through the bushes, he gave a low whistle, then called softly, "Good old Cherry! Good old girl, here I am at last!"

But Cherry was gone.

Chapter XIV

"The signal is one shot, then two, spaced."

IT was almost noon when Lance, dirty, hungry, sick-at-heart, limped slowly up the farm drive. Boney was the first of the Chapelles to reach him, but Lance hadn't a word for him. Nor a word for the twins who walked toward him, their eyes wide and solemn. His attention was all for M'ma Chapelle who stood in the doorway with an anxious expression on her face and an eager question on her lips. "Lance, where is—"

"I don't know," said Lance. "I just don't know. I've hunted and hunted—"

"But—come inside, Lance." As if she realized how completely worn out he was, M'ma Chapelle didn't say another word until she had led Lance into the kitchen, pushed him down on the bench beside the hearth, and brought him a dipper of water from the pail. Then, "You sure do look done-in, Lance. Oh, I don't suppose I can blame you. Only, whatever'll we do, Lance, if—? It's been hours already."

Lance swallowed the very last drop in the dipper, and then he spoke earnestly. "I'm going back again, ma'am. I'm going back right away and I'll cover every speck of ground between Valley Mill and Canady. It *was* my fault, Mrs. Chapelle. But I tied the rope tight. I *did* tie that rope tight and I don't see—"

134

He saw a puzzled look come into her white face. "Tied the rope? What rope? Whatever are you talkin' about, Lance?"

"Cherry, ma'am. I tied her fast to the limb of a maple. However, she broke loose—"

"It's Cherry you've been a-hunting?"

"Of course," nodded Lance. "Trying to pick up hoof prints. Once I was sure I had found some on this very road, but then I remembered how I had sometimes ridden her along it lately. What did you think I was hunting, ma'am?"

"Cherry's in the lean-to," said M'ma Chapelle wearily. "I'm talking about 'Tilda."

It was Lance's turn to stare in bewilderment. "Tilda?"

M'ma Chapelle reached into the pocket of her dress and brought out the scrap of yellow paper which Lance recognized as the note he had written the night before and left on Cherry's overturned feed bucket. In his realization that here was some sort of new trouble, Lance had hardly a thought to spare for the welcome news of Cherry's return. He took the note and saw beneath his own message the scrawled printing of Mathilde.

> "I AM GOING TO THE CLEARING
> TO MEET MR. SMARTY LANCE."

M'ma Chapelle sat down on the chair beside the table. " 'Tilda's been plain possessed to traipse to yore Clearing and into the Holler, too, ever since I can remember. Sometimes I've figgered she comes natural by a roamin' foot on account of my husband, Pierre. She must have gone right off when she found that note o' yourn afore I could stop her. I wasn't too worrit, thinking she'd meet you, but when Cherry come a-galloping home without neither one, I felt as if something had happened. And then you come alone. What I don't see, Lance, is—well, how you missed her. There's just a straight road to the Clearing after the fork."

"I didn't go to the Clearing," said Lance briefly. "I didn't even go to the Hollow. I—well, I went along the road by Squaw Hill a piece, and then I turned around and came back to where I'd tied Cherry. Then I spent a lot of time just looking for her."

Suddenly all the events of the night, the waiting at the entrance to the trail, the stalking of the men, the rendezvous in the forest with the wagoner "Dawes," seemed unreal and like episodes in a last year's nightmare. Here was a brand new and very serious problem to be faced. Where was Mathilde?

"If she doesn't come back pretty soon," said M'ma Chapelle simply, "I don't know just what to do. We're so far from help. If I were strong enough and Cherry fitten to ride, I'd go a-looking for her myself, but Cherry's been all of a-tremble ever since she came back. Too much so to eat her oats." She rose wearily, and going over to the big iron kettle hanging in the fireplace ladled out a bowl of corn mush.

"Eat that, Lance, and then we'll think what must be done." Walking to the window, she stared out at the road up which Mathilde ought to have returned many hours ago.

But Lance, hungry though he had been for a long time, pushed the bowl from him. "I must take a look at Cherry first," he said.

He found that M'ma Chapelle had been quite right. Cherry, for all she had come home to her own stall, was quivering throughout her entire little body and rolling her brown eyes. Lance threw his arms about her neck, pleased that she permitted him to do so. He could feel the trembling and twitching of muscles under the satiny skin.

"Oh, Cherry," he murmured, and laid his cheek against the little animal's shaggy mane. "How did you get loose? Did someone untie you? And why are you shaking so? Please stop shaking. Please eat your oats, Cherry!"

He stayed until at last it seemed to him that the little chestnut had actually grown more quiet. Then, feeling a very real gnawing in his own insides, he started back for the house and the bowl of mush.

As he did so, he felt a sudden surge of anger toward Mathilde. Weren't things bad enough without her making them worse? What business had she going to meet him anyhow? If she went only to the Clearing, she would undoubtedly find her way home again. If she kept on into the Hollow, she could easily get lost.

The corn meal mush tasted, it seemed to Lance, better than any food he had ever eaten, but even before he had finished it, he felt his head nodding, his eyes closing.

Dimly he realized that somebody—M'ma Chapelle, of course—was helping him to the old wooden settle that was backed against one side of the room, was pushing a pillow under him, was throwing something over him. After that he didn't remember anything for a long, long time.

> "Fort Dummer was named for Sir William, tra la!
> Fort Dummer was named for he—"

Lance stirred uneasily on the hard settle. I been dreaming I was back in Tin Peddler Joe's wagon, he thought with drowsy amusement. I can still hear that song of his ringing in my ears.

"Fort Dummer was named for Sir William, tra la—"

Lance sat up suddenly. Was he dreaming or wasn't he? Was there really somebody singing at the top of his lungs, or was he only imagining it? A double yell from both of the twins at once and a quick exclamation from M'ma Chapelle waked him completely, and with that awakening came the remembrance that Mathilde was gone. This excitement on the part of everybody around him must mean she had come back.

The next instant, hearing an unmistakable rumble of wheels, he knew the disturbance couldn't be 'Tilda. Or could it?

He was off the settle and out of the door, and all but bumped into two men who had just climbed down from the high seat of the wagon in which he had ridden so many pleasant miles. One of the men—the one he was very happy to see—wore perched on his left ear a scrap of hat with a perky red feather in it. The other was the man with the gray eyes who had ascended through the trap door into the attic of Mead's Inn.

The peddler took care of all introductions and explanations. Hurrying into the kitchen, after a hearty slap on the back for Lance, he bent low over M'ma Chapelle's hand.

"Ma'am, I'm right proud to meet the lady my young friend here spoke so highly of. I presume these two peas in a pod are your young uns? This gentleman, allow me to present him, ma'am, is my esteemed acquaintance, Hamilton Brandon, Esquire, of Rutland Village. He knows your kin, Miss Dilsie Buell. We run across each other in Valley Mill—"

But here Constable Brandon broke in to speak for himself. "Glad to know you, madam. There are a few little questions I want to put to your—let me see, I believe this lad is not your son?"

M'ma Chapelle spoke up quickly. "Lance is helping us until my husband returns, just like a real son," she explained. "I've only the twins here and 'Tilda." Suddenly her eyes filled. "Oh, I'm in such terrible trouble! My 'Tilda ran off this morning and hasn't come back. I'm that afraid. . . ." Here poor M'ma Chapelle broke down completely.

The two men looked at each other. Then each spoke at the same moment.

"Which way did she go, ma'am?" asked Tin Peddler Joe.

"My business can wait," said Constable Brandon. "Don't worry, ma'am. We'll find your girl."

But a few minutes later, headed for the wilderness which stretched in front of them, Lance had a feeling the constable was less confident than his words to M'ma Chapelle had implied. "Powerful big area for one young un to get lost in," he said grimly.

The three of them, Tin Peddler Joe, the constable, and Lance, were crowded into the front seat of the peddler's wagon. "We'll hitch Bag-o'-bones in the Clearing," Tin Peddler Joe had declared. "Then we'll spread out, every man for himself, three ways to once. Ain't too much time afore dark."

When they reached the Clearing, there was no sign of Mathilde. Lance had not expected there would be. No one, not even M'ma Chapelle, knew as well as he how possessed Mathilde was with the idea of visiting the Hollow. Never, she would figure, would she have a better chance to do that very thing than right now. And the fact that she would be expecting to catch up with him at every turn of the trail would no doubt lead her farther into the Hollow's depths than she realized.

Bag o' bones was left tied under the lean-to which was the only thing, except the trough for the spring, left standing of Lance's former home. Tin Peddler Joe let down the sides of his wagon and padlocked them. "Takin' no chances with the best outfit o' tin and ironware in the State o' Vermont," he explained.

"Better padlock your horse," suggested the constable. "Anyone a-looking for a good living could help himself to the hull outfit."

"I'll take a chance on that," retorted the peddler. "Who'd want the outfit with Bag o' bones thrown in?"

But Lance saw that he blanketed the horse carefully, adjusted a bit of harness, and gave her a farewell slap on her thin flank.

Once the three were started on the trail toward the Ridge there was little conversation, partly because they proceeded in single file, partly because each was intently listening for any sound, any call, and, perhaps most of all, because they felt the grimness of the situation. Each had secretly hoped to meet 'Tilda on her way back or to find her at the Clearing. Since neither hope had been realized, the only assumption must be that she was wandering somewhere in the wilderness of the Hollow.

When the top of the Ridge was reached, the constable made a suggestion. "Joe's idea of scattering in different directions strikes me as right proper to put in effect from now on. Foolish for all three to stick to the trail. Young 'un ain't really lost iffen she's on the trail. Likewise, at reg'lar intervals, each on us ought ter give a holler. Call her by name. What you say her name is?"

" 'Tilda," said Lance promptly. "And I'm heading to the left. I know a spot she might have tried to find." He could recall how one afternoon when he had been coaxing Mathilde to help him saddle Cherry, she had wormed out of him the story of his finding the copper coin in the mud by the brook near the grove of white birches.

"Kerrect. You head to the left. I'll swing to the right. Joe, you go straight without necessarily sticking to the trail. If any of us find her, the signal is one shot, then two, spaced, and the rest of us will go back to the Clearing. If we don't find her—"

Tin Peddler Joe interrupted him. "Afore we split, I got a little story to tell ye. A true one. Happened last day o' May, year 1780. I was a-peddlin' down in Sunderland, and I heerd him with my own two ears. A hundred or so neighbors were searchin' for Eldad Taylor's young 'uns, Kezziah and Betsey. Got themselves lost somewheres between the Battenkill and the Roarin' Branch. We'd hunted all one day, all the next, 'n up ter the middle o' the third day, when most on us voted to quit, as bein' no further use. And right then 'n there a powerful big giant of a man climbed onto a stump 'n with tears a-streamin' down his eyes told us how them pore young 'uns was hungry and a-cryin' for their pa 'n ma that very minute, and we was to keep a-goin' until we found 'em, and we did, a little afore night. Sure larned me my lesson, Ethan Allen did."

"Did—did you say Ethan Allen?" asked Lance. "The one who stood up to the Yorkers?"

"That I did, lad. And anything Ethan Allen says is

gospel to me." Tin Peddler Joe swung his flintlock across his shoulder. "We'll hunt the Chapelle young 'un 'til either we find *her* or a she bear gits *us*."

Chapter XV

"Hands up!"

NEITHER the grove of white birch nor the banks of Copper Coin Brook yielded any glimpse of the lost Mathilde. Although Lance called her name over and over again, as he could hear the others doing until he had gone beyond the sound of their voices, there came no answer. Perhaps, he couldn't help thinking, she was safe at home by now, not having gone as far as the Hollow at all. Or, if she had, having cut back to the road through the woods while her searchers were following the trail to the Ridge.

Gradually, however, there began to be moments when he was overwhelmed with a panicky fear that night would fall without 'Tilda being found. At such moments he would begin to run, yelling at the top of his lungs, " 'Tilda! 'Tilda! Oh, 'Tilda!"

It was during one of these moments he very nearly missed the first bit of evidence that anyone but himself had been in that vicinity. He was following a narrow deer-path when he saw that a branch on a black birch tree had been broken off short. He stopped calling and stood still, looking about for the rest of the branch. He found it, not under the tree, but several yards ahead on the trail, and when he picked it up he saw that the bark had been nibbled for several inches. Instantly he recalled

'Tilda's fondness for birch bark and the fact that she never failed to stop at a certain black birch on the edge of the pasture for a "bit of something to chew on."

The tell-tale branch in his hand, Lance stared ahead along the trail that was scarcely a foot in width, and it seemed to him that all the bushes and boughs had a look as though someone had pushed through them not very long ago. He studied the trail at his feet and, although the ground was too spongy to retain an ordinary foot-print, he fancied one clump of moss bore an impress like that which would be made by the heel of one of 'Tilda's boots.

He was about to shout her name again, when he heard a noise. At first he was not sure just what sort of noise it was. A voice? A hammer blow? Something falling? Perhaps it was a mixture of all three. All he knew certainly was that it came from deep within the woods on his left and not in the direction toward which he was going.

Then he heard it again, and this time it seemed to be from some sort of work being carried on. Suddenly the possible significance of the sounds flashed over him. Had he succeeded in doing by chance what he had long sought to do deliberately? Had he found the hidden retreat of the men who, by carrying on some nefarious business of their own, had turned the wild and lovely Hollow into a place of evil mystery?

He forgot for a moment why he was where he was, forgot the lost Mathilde, turned to plunge into the woods in the direction from which the sounds had come. Then he remembered. I've got to find 'Tilda first, he thought dully. I can't do anything else. When I do find her, if I do, I'll come back.

Yet he made no movement to go, as if a realization of what he was foregoing kept him rooted to the spot. They sound as if they were packing in a hurry to get out, he reflected. They think they are being hunted. Even if I should find 'Tilda soon and come back, it will be too late. If I could only creep up on them now, old Eagle-eye and I, and surprise them—

Lance could see as plain as day the three men walking in front of him single file along the trail, hands high above their heads. He could see them herded into the Clearing until Tin Peddler Joe and the constable returned, then padlocked into the peddler's wagon and taken to Valley Mill to tell their story and reveal the nature of their mysterious enterprise. To do all that would be to complete the task he and his father had set out to do. Wasn't it, he reasoned, as important to rid the State of Vermont of a secret menace as to find, a little sooner than she would otherwise be found, an annoying person like 'Tilda who had wilfully put herself in an unpleasant situation? And why, he thought bitterly, was he always having to decide between two courses of action? Was it going to be like that all his life?

Twice he started into the woods, then slowly, reluctantly, resumed his way along the trail. After a moment he began to run and soon could hear the sounds no more.

Ten minutes later he came upon Mathilde. She was sitting on a large flat rock eating blackberries from a cup made of an oak leaf. Her mouth was stained with berry juice, her boots were caked with mud, and her dress was torn in a dozen places.

When she saw Lance, she frowned. "It's about time," she said crossly. "I was beginning to think I'd never find you."

Lance swallowed. He was moved by a strange feeling which he supposed must be relief. At the same time he had the strangest desire to shake 'Tilda until her teeth rattled. And he kept thinking of things to say and then deciding he'd better not say them.

Finally, "Listen to me, 'Tilda," he managed to get out with reasonable calmness. "You've been bound you'd get mixed up with my trying to find out what's been going on in the Hollow. That's why you ran away this morning, isn't it?"

"What do you 'spose *is* going on?" asked 'Tilda, ignoring Lance's question and continuing to pop one fat berry after another into her mouth.

"Nothing, probably," said Lance sadly. "Not any more. But I can't be dead sure, and so you've got to do exactly as I say."

"I will, Lance!" 'Tilda, finding something exciting in Lance's final words, slid down from the rock.

Lance told her quickly about the noises he had heard. "I want to get as close to them as I can, if they're still there—the men, I mean," he said. "I want you to stand where I tell you to in case I need old Eagle-eye which you'll be holding for me. Do you understand?"

"Of course I do. I'm not stupid."

"Very well, then. Follow me." Lance started back over the trail on a dog trot.

He was afraid both that the noises would have ceased altogether or that he would pass the spot where he had heard them before, and he paid little attention as to whether 'Tilda was following him or not. He was therefore startled when she suddenly hissed almost in his very ear, "I hear something! I really do!"

Lance stopped instantly to listen. "I hear it too!" he whispered. "The men are still there, and I'm going to get as close to them as I can!"

"I'm coming, too!" said 'Tilda promptly.

The going through the underbrush was slow and difficult, especially where each—and 'Tilda was as cautious as Lance—sought to avoid even the crackling of a single twig. Once 'Tilda, stepping into a patch of snow left from the recent storm, plunged through the crust nearly to her knees, but scrambled out so quickly Lance didn't know anything had happened.

The sounds grew louder and the voices more distinct as they pushed ahead. Suddenly, Lance caught a glimpse through the trees in front of him of a figure moving about, and realized that if he kept on he would soon come out into a clearing. He stopped where he was, and held up his hand to halt 'Tilda also.

Then, step by step, from tree to tree, he edged as near to the fringe of the clearing as he dared, and gazed eagerly at the scene in front of him.

Trees had been felled and underbrush hacked away in front of a rocky ledge. At the base of this ledge there was an opening which might, or might not—Lance couldn't tell from where he stood—be of considerable depth. A few yards from the opening stood a huge fireplace in which great fires must have burned, since the stones of which it was built were all heavily sooted and many of them were split. Beside the fireplace were three bulky bundles, either of blankets or of articles wrapped in blankets. Lance decided they were probably the latter, judging from the knobs and protuberances on them.

Suddenly his spine stiffened. The figure of a man came out of the opening below the rocky ledge, followed by another. The first was the man with the weasel-fur cap, the other, one of the two men Lance had seen with him on the trail.

Neither man appeared to be armed and instantly Lance wished he had old Eagle-eye. He looked back for 'Tilda and to his surprise found that while he had been staring at the clearing she had crept so close behind him that his musket was within reach.

He was on the point of stretching out his hand for it, with half a plan formed in his mind of walking out to confront the pair and demand their surrender, when he remembered something. There was a third man to be reckoned with. Where was he?

While he hesitated, one of the men—not the one with the weasel-fur cap—jerked his thumb in the direction of the cave. "What you aimin' ter do with him?" he asked.

"Him?" growled the other. "Ontie him so's he kin start us on the trail west, arter which he kin starve ter death, fur's I'm consarned. Git yer pack up the ledge. Then come back 'n git yore gun."

Lance watched while each of the men shouldered one of the bundles beside the fireplace, made his way up a narrow path that climbed the almost perpendicular face of the ledge, and disappeared into the heavy growth of cedars on the top. His mind was working rapidly. "They'll come back for their guns and to untie their comrade who must have crossed them. He seems to know how to get out of the Hollow by some way they don't. If he's in the cave, tied up, I can get their guns without his hindering me, and maybe, if he's angered at them, he wouldn't hinder me anyhow. And it's my last chance. My very last chance."

He grabbed old Eagle-eye from 'Tilda and then, forgetting her, broke from cover and started to run across the clearing. He had reached the mouth of the cave when he heard a yell. He turned to see the man with the weasel-fur hat on his way back down the ledge. Realized the man had seen him. Realized too that 'Tilda had followed him. That pest of a 'Tilda—

"Get into that cave, 'Tilda!" he ordered, lifting old

Eagle-eye quickly to his shoulder. "Get into that cave and stay there!"

Then he took a step forward. "Hands up!" he said, and was surprised to find his voice calm and steady. The man with the weasel-fur cap, who had reached the ground, lifted his arms slowly above his head, an ugly look on his evil face. At the same moment, behind him, Lance saw a second man descending the cliff. It was not, however, the same man he had seen before in the clearing. It was the "third man" he had been wondering about and had assumed, from what he overheard, was bound and helpless within the cave.

In another instant, the other man, who had climbed the cliff with the pack, would return. Three against himself and old Eagle-eye. Suppose they rushed him—

Even as he watched both men and held his musket steady he heard a wild scream from the cave behind him, and knew it to be 'Tilda's.

Chapter XVI

"More than anything else in the world—"

So appalled was Lance at the sound of 'Tilda's scream that for an instant he couldn't have moved if he had tried; and in that brief span of time something of what she was saying communicated itself to him. It kept him from forgetting all about the man he faced and going to her rescue from snake or bat or whatever it was which he felt must have frightened her.

Of course what she was saying didn't make a particle of sense.

"P'pa Chapelle! P'pa Chapelle! Mon père! P'pa! D'ou viens tu? P'pa!" That crazy 'Tilda.

But to the evil-faced man coming toward Lance with his arms held high above his head, the words seemed to carry a meaning, for, when he was within a few feet of Lance he spoke. "Iffen it isn't Mr. Busybody! Along with Frenchie's brat. And along of a musket, too. What might you be aimin' to do, Mr. Busybody, iffen I might ask it?"

Lance could see one man behind the speaker. He could hear sounds from the ledge that seemed to indicate that the man who had gone first with one of the bulky packages, was descending, but he did not dare turn away his eyes to make sure. Was it possible the man in front of the muzzle of old Eagle-eye was quite aware of the nearness of his two companions and thought, if he could win a

little delay, they would somehow outmaneuver his cap-
tor?

"Stop where you are!" said Lance.

"Iffen I don't choose to stop . . ." But he did stop, his
eyes narrowing as if calculating his chances of springing
at Lance before he could fire.

Then Lance heard at his side a breathless voice which
certainly wasn't 'Tilda's.

"Tres bien. Me, I'm here. Pierre. Pierre Chapelle.
Mathilde—she 'ave ontie me. Now I keep theese gun
from cave aimed on that fellow behin' that fellow you
'ave aimed at. Mathilde—she point with other gun I also
find at that fellow coming down cleef. Come queekly
down, mon ami! Soon, Lance, we weel march all those
fellows to farm for the good M'ma to see weeth own
eyes why P'pa he tak so long reech home."

So 'Tilda had not been crazy after all! She had actually
found Pierre Chapelle, her father, in that cave! Although
this was no time to hear the story of how he came to be
there, it was enough for Lance that Pierre had immediately grasped the situation, and was ready to help capture
the men.

Suddenly Lance remembered there was other assistance
he could count on.

"Fire once into the air, wait a minute, and then fire
twice," he told Pierre. "It's a signal."

"The three of you," Lance told the men, "will walk
one behind the other, your hands tied."

So it was that, after a tedious retracing of the trail,

through the gathering twilight, never for an instant daring to relax their vigilance, Lance and Pierre and 'Tilda delivered the three men to Constable Brandon.

It was decided that Lance should drive, with Pierre and 'Tilda on the seat beside him. The others would walk, one on either side of the wagon, since Bag o' bones, pulling a heavier load than he had ever pulled before, would make slow going of it. And while they journeyed thus through the night, Lance listened to Pierre's story.

"I reech thees State o' Vermont t'ree, four weeks ago. Mebbe seex, I dunno. I am in so great hurree see my leetle Jean and Jacques, Mathilde, M'ma Chapelle, I tak short cut over Mountain through Hollow. Een that Hollow I run smack into these—how you say eet?—jail birds. They verree busy mekking money. Fine, beeg shiny copper money. Got plenty 'queepment. Beeg lot copper. Roller machine. Dies. Plenty everyt'ing lak you see wrapped up in blankets to pack out. Mekking fine lot o' money."

"Making money!" exclaimed Lance. "Making money!" So that was it. That was the mystery of the Hollow, and it was every bit as ugly and evil a one as he, and his father, too, had felt it would turn out to be.

"Mekking plenty money. I leesten to them talk. How they peek so lonely places where no one he ever come, and how they keep changing that place. They do not like that I know what bad beezness they do, so they tie me fast. They tell me I may go when they ready also to leave. Mebbe so. Mebbe not. They tell me first I mus' show to them the way how I 'ave come. They weesh leave by that same way. And all the time I eating jus' deer meat and I am keep tied weeth rope."

"But I did untie you, mon père!" squealed 'Tilda, and would have bounced on the seat if she hadn't been wedged so tightly between Lance and her father.

"You 'ave ontie me, mon petit chou," agreed her father fondly, "and I could reach guns those evil men stand in corner of cave."

'Tilda, whom her father had just called his "dear little cabbage," drew a deep breath of happiness. P'pa Chapelle was home at last from his wanderings, and she had actually had a share both in his rescue and in the solving of the mystery of the Hollow. There was nothing more she wanted of life, except a bowl of hot oat porridge from the big kettle over the fireplace, and a crisp, brown journeycake from the oven beside it.

Lance, on the other hand, felt queer, quite as if he had been leaning against a fence and someone had taken it away without warning. For months he had thought and thought and thought about the mystery of the Hollow and now—well, there just wasn't any more mystery. For weeks he had felt responsible for the Chapelles and now— well, their welfare was no longer his concern. For hours 'Tilda had been lost in the wilderness—and here she was, pert and lively as ever, perched on the seat beside him. In short, Lance's world had suddenly up-ended.

He tried to readjust it while 'Tilda and her father, both chattering at once in a funny mixture of French and

English, exchanged excited accounts of all that had taken place during their long separation.

I'm free now, he thought. But free for what? Well, for one thing, to get a job in the Iron Works at Bennington. Yet to Lance, a job, necessary and important though it would be, didn't seem at the moment an adequate substitute for the mystery which had occupied both his waking thoughts and his dreams.

And suddenly that which had been pushed into the back of his mind by the pressure of other things, came into the front of it, and he knew what he wanted above anything else in the whole world. He wanted a horse of his own, a little bay horse like Farmer Bob Evans' with quicksilver in his heels.

Bit by bit a plan pieced itself together in his mind.

"You'll be coming to Valley Mill with us in the morning," Constable Brandon had told him. "You are the one responsible for tracking down this bunch o' swindlers we've been trailing for nigh on two years. Your evidence will be wanted."

He would go to Valley Mill with Constable Brandon and do whatever was expected of him. Then, when that duty was done, he would hurry out to Bob Evans' farm to put the matter squarely before him. "Let me work for you without pay until I've earned twice as much as you think Figure is worth, Mr. Evans. I'll work overtime for nothing. I'll work like—like anything."

But how stupid of him! Farmer Evans didn't have anything to say about it. Figure didn't belong to him. Very well, I'll find out where the owner lives. Lance almost spoke the words aloud. "I'll go to his house, and I'll say to him..."

All the way home Lance carried on his imaginary conversations. They made him forget that Bag o' bones maintained a gait hardly faster than that of Wash and Jeff, that he was hungry as a bear after hibernation, that he had slept hardly at all for forty-eight hours.

It was well past midnight when the farm was reached. Lance saw at once that M'ma Chapelle must have heard the wheels of the wagon long before it turned into the drive, for she was standing in the open doorway staring out into the night, an old cloak of P'pa Chapelle's thrown about her shoulders.

At 'Tilda's wild scream, "We found P'pa! We found P'pa all tied up in a cave with guns!," M'ma gave a scream herself, almost as wild as 'Tilda's. She ran across the yard, not noticing that the cloak fell to the ground, seeing only P'pa Chapelle as he jumped from the wagon with 'Tilda falling out behind him.

For a long time after they had gone into the house and M'ma Chapelle was setting out porridge and journey-cakes, she seemed to be able to say little else, over and over, than, "I was that worried they wouldn't bring 'Tilda back to me, and they brought the two of you! God has been good to us."

For what was left of the night Constable Brandon and Tin Peddler Joe took turn and turn about watching their three prisoners who had been given food, water to drink, and beds in the haymow.

Lance wanted his share of standing guard, but the constable refused. "No, lad, ye've already done a complete job on 'em, and ye've earned the rest ye missed last night.

"I doubt if they try to get away," he went on. "They're gamblers. The game is up and they know it. Howsoe'er, 'tain't only for onlawful minting o' coin they'll be tried, nor for stealing sheets o' copper to make their onlawful money out of. There's a kidnapping charge added to their other misdeeds, so they might try making a bolt of it. Joe here and myself, we'll see to it they don't git a chance. Arter we finish with 'em in Valley Mill, we'll likely be asked to cart 'em in to Rutland. When that's over, we'll be ready to pick up that driver o' the load o' pearl ash you was a-telling of when he goes to keep his rendyvoos at Danby Jake's.

"Ye've rid the State o' Vermont of a pest worser 'n the smallpox plague, lad. But don't keep me here talking. Git ter yer rest."

Lance, who had been afraid he would fall asleep while he listened, stumbled drowsily, gratefully back to the kitchen where M'ma Chapelle had made up a bed for him on the settle. Two minutes after he crawled in among the blankets he was so deep in slumber a volley of cannon would not have wakened him. .

Chapter XVII

"I've known strange things to happen on Fair Day."

"THIS is nice!" beamed M'ma Chapelle next morning, as she hurried from one to the other with steaming flapjacks hot from the soapstone griddle. "This *is* nice." Lance, watching her, knew that P'pa Chapelle's return and 'Tilda's being found had been better medicine than any herb, simple, or drug a doctor could have prescribed.

" 'Tis very nice indeed, ma'am," agreed Tin Peddler Joe. "I'm an old hand at the flapjack myself, but I'll have ter admit yer quite my equ'il."

"I mean it's nice having so many at the table," explained M'ma Chapelle. " 'Tis a lonely spot here. We never have company."

"Only Lance," spoke up 'Tilda, "and he's stopped being company."

"You are so right, my leetle one!" exclaimed Pierre quickly. "Thees good Lance he ees not companee. He ees—how you say eet?—a most filial lad. He has been lak a son to M'ma. And that ees why, w'en we do that which we shall soon do so M'ma will nevair again be lonelee, we shall ask Lance one leetle question, and he weel surely say, 'Yes,' I theenk, and then . . ." But here P'pa Chapelle gave a shrug of his shoulders, twisted his funny little black moustache, smiled slyly, and refused to say another word.

Lance, bewildered, saw from M'ma Chapelle's expression that she had no more idea than he what her husband was talking about. 'Tilda too stared at her father, and even Tin Peddler Joe held the pitcher of maple syrup suspended in mid-air for a second. Only the twins, who were very busy having a contest as to which could eat the greater number of flapjacks, did not realize that anything unusual had been said.

What question, wondered Lance, could P'pa Chapelle possibly ask to which he would so surely answer yes?

A few minutes later the peddler rose from the table. "Constable will be a-needing of me to help put those scamps back into the wagon," he said. "I do thank ye kindly, ma'am, for yer hospitality, and seeing as how a mite more space in the wagon wouldn't be amiss, I'm asking ye to accept of a pair o' my largest copper kittles. Ye'll find 'em right handy, ma'am, when it comes ter—" and here Lance saw him wink at Pierre— "packing things, should ye ever move on." Then, before M'ma Chapelle could utter a word, he made her a low, quick bow with his hand on his heart, and was gone.

"Packing things." What did Tin Peddler Joe mean by that?

But Lance had other matters to attend to which soon made him forget the puzzling remarks he had heard. It had been decided that he and P'pa Chapelle, both of whom it seemed would be needed to give information about the prisoners, would drive to Valley Mill in the ox cart, following the constable and the peddler who would go in the wagon with the three men.

'Tilda begged to accompany them. "Lance always gets to go!" she complained.

"Tais-toi, Mathilde!" P'pa Chapelle said sharply. "Be quiet. Eet weel be you shall get plentee rides some one of these fine days. Stay with M'ma." And' 'Tilda knew better than to say anything more.

Before yoking Wash and Jeff, Lance did the usual round of morning chores. Cherry, to his great relief, was like her old self. Lance slipped the halter over her head and hitched her outside, while he cleaned her stall and brought fresh bedding.

Constable Brandon chose that very moment to lead one of his prisoners to the peddler's wagon. The man stared first at Cherry, then at Lance, and then back at Cherry. Then he gave an ugly laugh. "Iffen yonder little devil hadn't broken loose," he snarled, "arter I untied her, we'd a-gotten clear away afore ye caught us, dang her hide!"

So that was what had happened! Lance saw it all very clearly. The two men, returning from their rendezvous with the driver of the load of potash, had heard Cherry's restless whinny in the underbrush where Lance had tied her. They had found and freed her, and would have ridden her back through the Hollow to use in packing out their equipment had not Cherry managed somehow to break away. As Lance's discovery of them before they disappeared for good had been a matter of split seconds, he now said to himself that perhaps he had really the little colt to thank for that capture of the counterfeiters. Good girl, Cherry!

The ride to Valley Mill seemed endless to Lance, so impatient was he to talk to Farmer Bob Evans.

P'pa Chapelle alternated between spells of incessant chatter and even longer ones of deep silence. Once or twice he seemed on the point of putting a question to Lance—only apparently to think better of it.

When he did talk, he told with enthusiasm of the rolling country in York State through which he had journeyed; of the persons he had met there; of the bold project, even now being discussed in their legislature, of draining the Great Lakes into the Hudson River through a narrow waterway with locks in it, so that boats could travel from one end to the other, pulled by mules on the bank.

About the latter, "Eet ees a dream too beeg for a man to accompleesh," he said, "but a veree beeg dream for a man to dream."

Lance listened with a small part of his mind. With the rest he made exciting plans for himself which were to start just as soon as the constable was through with him. Now and then he drew a long, deep breath, and straightened his shoulders. It was good in a way to be free of the mystery, just as it was good to be free of the Chapelles, although he no longer thought of them as "those Chapelles." They had come to be individuals whom he liked.

The day was mild, and the sun felt agreeably warm on his face. A soft haze lay on the mountains. The snow, which had fallen the night he came back from Rutland Village, had gone, except for an occasional patch on the north side of boulder or hummock. Only the gay flags of crimson, scarlet, and gold run up by the maples proclaimed the fact that autumn had come.

On reaching Valley Mill, Lance and Pierre found that the constable and the peddler had arrived much earlier.

The wagon was standing in front of the Fish and Turtle, and Tin Peddler Joe himself was waiting beside it, the red feather in his scrap of hat bobbing gently in the breeze.

" 'Tis all ready for ye they be," he told them. "Simon Chittenden being constable for Valley Mill, they're a-using of his back room for court. Allow me to escort ye both inside."

The "back room" proved little more than a narrow ell, jutting from the kitchen. The small amount of light which made its way through the tiny—and very dirty—panes of the single window showed Simon and Constable Brandon seated on a wooden settle. The three prisoners, silent and sullen, their arms bound behind them, slumped on three stools.

Lance was called upon at once to tell his story from

the very first time he and his father had seen the stooped figures climbing the crest of the Ridge in the moonlight to his final capture of them at their hiding-place in the Hollow.

"Persistent lad ye be," was Simon's comment when Lance was through. "Kept at 'em. Got 'em in the end. Persistent, I say."

"May I go now?" Lance, who had already heard Pierre's story several times, was eager to be about his own business.

Simon looked at Constable Brandon, who nodded briefly.

"I geev you one leetle hour, mon ami," spoke up Pierre. "Then we mus' return—you and I—to M'ma and les petits from whom I 'ave already been too much away. And besides thees night I 'ave one beeg surprise! So I geev you one leetle hour."

Lance was off like a shot, down the dusty street, across the covered bridge, along the winding road that dipped and rose and dipped again on its way to the Evans farm.

P'pa Chapelle can't have any surprise to do with me, he was thinking as he went. Perhaps I won't even be going back with him. Perhaps Farmer Evans will let me start right in working for him to earn money with which to buy Figure.

He found the farmer still hard at work, clearing the primeval forest out of his dooryard. And, just as before, the little bay stallion was standing patiently until it was time to snake away the logs which had been felled.

Farmer Evans, at sight of Lance, held out his hand. "You did a right good job," he said.

Lance looked puzzled, but shook hands heartily.

"Catching those varmints," went on the farmer. "The State o' Vermont is much obleeged to you. News travels fast in these parts, and what you've done is already spreading four ways."

But Lance hadn't come to talk about something which was over and done with. Nor could he bring himself to beat about the bush. "Mr. Evans," he said hurriedly, "you told me once you didn't own Figure. You—you haven't bought him since I last saw you, have you?"

The farmer gave Lance a friendly smile. "You sure have an interest in the little fellow. "No, it's as I said before. His owner won't sell."

Perhaps the expression on Lance's face showed how disappointing the information was to him. Perhaps the farmer felt an impulse to act kindly toward the lad who had done the whole countryside a favor. "Sit down on this log," he said, "and let's talk things over. Do you remember my mentioning Fair Day?"

Lance nodded. "Yes," he said. "I do."

"That's five days away. It's going to be a big day. Biggern' ever this year. Always is. Figure's owner, that Randolph fiddler, sent word to me he's coming down. Seems there's been a lot o' gossip about this little horse o' his'n being so powerful, and he's been egged into entering him in a log-hauling contest. Now I've got a hunch that if Figure loses, you or I or anyone can buy him for a song, but if he wins—well, the whole o' Valley Mill couldn't raise enough for his purchase."

Lance didn't say anything for a long time. Then, "Do you think he will win?" he asked soberly.

The farmer threw out his hands. "Your guess is as good as mine, lad. 'Twill be a stiff trial. Common sense tells me the little horse is too small, too gentle-like, to stand up to real competition. On the other hand, there's something about him . . ." Farmer Bob looked thoughtfully at the sleek, chunky body of the little animal. Then he rose to his feet. "Better be on hand, lad, for the contest. I've known strange things to happen on Fair Day."

A few minutes later, after several wistful glances back at Figure, Lance was on his way to find P'pa Chapelle.

Supper at the farm was over. The pewter plates and mugs had been washed and put away in the corner cupboard. M'ma Chapelle had set her buckwheat batter to rise, and Lance, who still felt that he had more sleep coming to him, was on the point of turning in for the night, when P'pa Chapelle rose from his seat by the hearth and took his stand in the middle of the room. His black eyes were twinkling, and his whole face wore a pleased expression.

M'ma Chapelle and 'Tilda and even the twins knew from their father's manner that he was excited over something, and so they were excited, too. Lance, who could not imagine P'pa Chapelle's having anything to say which would affect him, was mildly curious.

"So now eet ees that I 'ave a surprise," began Pierre,

rubbing his two hands together, and bobbing his head up and down as he spoke. "A beeg surprise. For Lance also. You theenk old P'pa Pierre, he 'ave the eetching foot. Mebbe so. Mebbe so. And a good theeng sometimes to 'ave. Because he 'ave thees eetching foot, we are leave thees State o' Vermont, the so-cold mountains and so-late spreengs, w'ere M'ma she ees always lonelee. We move to spot in York state. I 'ave paid money on that spot just w'ere that so-beeg deetch weel be dug, eef eet ees ever dug anyw'ere. Neighbors so near M'ma can at all times see smokes from chimney. So now we pack in one, two, t'ree days before more snow she come. And Lance he weel go, too, as our so good son. Ees eet not so, M'ma?"

For a moment no one, not even 'Tilda, said one single word. Then everyone did something at once. The twins jumped up and down. 'Tilda gave a wild whoop and threw her arms about her father's neck. M'ma Chapelle drew a long, deep breath. Lance rose to his feet, thrust his hands into his breeches pockets, and swallowed once or twice.

P'pa Chapelle patted M'ma's shoulder, but watched Lance. "That ees fine chance for young man," he said.

"I—I don't like Yorkers," said Lance shortly.

"That ees long over weeth!" Pierre's tone was impatient.

Of course, Lance's common sense told him, P'pa Chapelle was right. The differences between Vermonters and Yorkers were things of the past. P'pa Chapelle was right, too, about it's being an opportunity for a boy to be offered a home. Then why did he hesitate? And why did he feel again that irritation at being called upon to make a decision? It was plain to see his whole life was going to consist of making decisions!

He knew M'ma Chapelle's glance was upon him. So was 'Tilda's. He must give some reply.

"Thank you very much," he said slowly. "If you don't go until after Fair Day, I will know better what to do."

"Fair Day?" Pierre frowned, then beamed. "I 'ave forgot. That weel be so good a day to sell our Amanda the sow. M'ma, we weel all go to Valley Mill to that Fair! And Lance he shall tell us then how he weel decide to say, 'Yes.'"

Once more the twins jumped up and down, and M'ma Chapelle was smiling.

"I never did think," said 'Tilda softly, and quite to herself, "I'd get to go to the Fair!"

"If Figure will only lose in the log-hauling match, I won't have to bother my head to decide," thought Lance. "I'll know exactly what to do!"

Chapter XVIII

"Must I think it over?"

"Move over, Jacques, and make room for my foot!"

" 'Tis a right pretty day for the Fair!"

"Move over, Jean, and make room for my other foot!"

"Tais-toi, Mathilde!"

Lance, standing beside Cherry, watched Wash and Jeff and the ox cart move slowly out into the road. On the seat, very straight, sat M'ma and P'pa Chapelle, dressed in their best. Behind, in the cart, were 'Tilda, the twins, and Amanda the sow. In a moment he too, mounted on Cherry, would be on his way to Valley Mill and the Fair.

As the ox cart disappeared down the road, hidden almost at once by the trees on either side, Lance looked about him deliberately. This might be the very last time he ever saw the small weathered farmhouse, the meadows sloping to the Little Pasture on the hilltop, the mountains in the distance with the wild reaches of the Hollow lying between. On the day after tomorrow the Chapelles would leave for that bit of land in York State not far from Uticy, which Pierre had taken to calling "the West." ("Veree soon now, mes petits, we weel mek our start for the West!") If Lance decided to go with them, he would return here after the Fair, but if he decided otherwise. . . . But why think about it now before he knew what the day would bring forth? Hadn't Farmer Bob said he'd known strange things to happen on Fair Day?

"Come on, Cherry!" he exclaimed aloud. "Let's be going!"

It had been Pierre's idea that Lance ride the little chestnut to Valley Mill. "Weeth Amanda in the ox wagon, there weel be too leetle room, Lance, for you and les petits. You weel ride on Cherry, for whom it will be good. Onlee do not gallop her too much at the first and at the last; mebbe a leetle in the middle."

But it was all Lance could do to obey P'pa Chapelle's orders. Cherry, who had had little exercise since her mad dash home from the rim of the Hollow, was filled with the wildest of spirits and could not, for a mile or two, be coaxed into anything slower than a lively trot, and at Lance's slightest movement of leg or body was off like a March wind. She passed the ox cart in a cloud of dust.

At this rate, thought Lance, I'll reach Valley Mill before the Fair really opens. And that is exactly what he did.

No sooner was he through the covered bridge, which Cherry first shied at, then took in nervous caperings, than he saw that great preparations were under way on the grassy meadow across the road from Bascom Brothers' Store.

A score of wooden booths had been erected, in and out of which milled men and women, children, babies, and dogs. Clouds of dust, stirred up by many feet, drifted over their heads. Rush baskets heaped with eggs, butter firkins, huge round cheeses, kegs, carts with and without the creatures which had drawn them thither from many miles around—all stood about at random as if their owners had suddenly gone away and left them forever.

In the midst of all the confusion, however, a certain progress was being made.

Standing on a barrel, an ugly little man with curly black hair was finishing some charcoal lettering on a slab of wood: DOC RAWSON'S GENUINE AND UN-SURPASSED TINCTURE WILL CURE RHEU-MATICS, SWOONING, LOWNESS OF SPIRITS, BRUISES, JAUNDICE, DOG-BITE— On the counter of the booth beneath him stood row upon row of tall bottles filled with a black liquid.

"That's Doc Rawson o' Philadelphy himself," Lance heard some one say. "Hops around from fair to fair like a flea on a yaller dog."

In the booth on the right, two women in shawls were

arranging an exhibit of home-made straw bonnets on tall wooden pegs.

In the booth on the left, half-a-dozen women were trying one way after another of displaying to the greatest advantage strips of material beneath a sign which read, "Special premiums for best pieces of dressed flannel."

From the rear of all the booths, discordant bleatings and lowings and cacklings and crowings and gruntings told where the live stock to be exhibited was being corralled. And down the road that very minute a litter of squealing pigs was being driven to join their fellows, already penned.

Lance drew a deep breath. The sooner he hitched Cherry in a safe and quiet spot, the sooner he could walk about and look things over. Also, while it was certain the Chapelles would not arrive for several hours, he would be much freer to roam as he pleased without the twins and 'Tilda at his heels.

He left Cherry in the grove beside the grist mill; several teams, hitched and blanketed, were already standing there.

Miller Robins, whose wheel had been turning since sunup, leaned in the doorway of the mill. "Handsome creature," he said, nodding toward Cherry. "Run across Bob Evans yet?"

"No," said Lance. "Why?"

"He's got the Randolph fiddler with him. Owner of the little bay. Come to see the log-hauling match, wagers on which are running high, wide, and handsome. Some claim he can't be beat by any horse in the State o' Vermont. Nonsense, I say. The little horse may be good, but not that good."

So Figure's owner had come exactly as Farmer Evans had expected he would!

Suddenly nothing in the whole Fair seemed to Lance of any importance except the log-hauling match. He wished it weren't so many hours away. He wished he could look into the future and see how the match was going to turn out. He wished . . . Slowly he walked back to the booths in the meadow.

"Lance! O, Lance! M'ma! P'pa! There's Lance!"

Lance, two hours later, was seated on the edge of the long porch running along the front of Bascom Brothers' General Store, eating dried whortleberries and drinking apple juice (he had found both on sale at the same booth), when he heard the excited voice of 'Tilda. Turning his head, he saw the stolid forms of Wash and Jeff only a few yards away, with 'Tilda standing up in the wagon.

"M'ma! P'pa! Did you ever see so many people? Look at the big banner between the trees! 'Valley Mill Fair', it says. Look at those two boys running a race with their feet in a sack! Look at those hundreds of oxen! What are you eating, Lance? I'm hungry!"

Lance stood up. He knew that P'pa Chapelle would need his help right away in ousting Amanda the sow from her pile of straw in the cart. Amanda's weight was more than half that of all the Chapelles put together, and that weight, plus a strong mind of her own, meant it would be no easy matter to transfer her from the wagon to a pen with a "Sow for Sale" sign on it.

By the time Lance had taken two steps, 'Tilda and the twins had jumped out, and P'pa Chapelle was helping M'ma Chapelle down from her seat.

It proved as hard to budge Amanda as Lance had foreseen. Then, all of a sudden, half-a-dozen bystanders realized that somebody was having some sort of difficulty with something and rushed over to help. In less than the twinkling of an eye the sow was out of the cart and into a wooden enclosure, and P'pa Chapelle was getting a nail from this one, a hammer from that, and a brush dipped in black stuff from still another. Soon, there, plain as day for everyone to read, was a sign that said, "Sow for sale. Owner, P. Chapelle."

Dinner, packed by M'ma Chapelle in a stone crock to keep moist, was eaten under the same butternut tree on the bank of the creek where Lance and 'Tilda had lunched on their earlier visit to Valley Mill. It was swallowed hastily, since no one wanted to waste any time with so much to see and do.

On their way back to the meadow, P'pa Chapelle and Lance—M'ma and 'Tilda and the twins had hurried ahead—stopped beside Amanda's pen. Three men were waiting for "Owner—P. Chapelle." Lance listened for a while to the six-way conversation among the four of them, then turned away. Had he been wrong in thinking P'pa Chapelle was eager to sell the sow? It certainly seemed so as Pierre hesitated, shrugged his shoulders, threw out his hands, and finally named a price with apparent reluctance.

Lance had not yet laid eyes on Farmer Evans, much as he wanted to do so, since Miller Robins had said Figure's owner was with him. Perhaps both men were busy making arrangements for the coming match.

Lance lingered to watch the judging of the yearlings, then made his way among the booths and their patrons to the road. There, as far as the eye could see, and even beyond the covered bridge, a line of oxen was waiting to take part in "the greatest, the most colossal, the most stupendous event of the day, the Valley Mill Agricultural Society ox parade!"

'Tilda had really been exaggerating when she spoke of "hundreds" of oxen, yet Lance had not supposed there were as many oxen in the whole State of Vermont as he now gazed upon. Nor had he realized that oxen came in so many different colors: red, white, brown, black, red and white, brown and white, black and white, and varying shades between.

As he stared, one of the drivers prodded with his goad the flank of the near ox of the front pair, and the long procession began a slow motion toward the reviewing stand, which had been set up at the Fish and Turtle. Two by two, two by two, they came, while the air resounded with the "Gees" and "Haws" and "Gits" from the owners, who seemed to be marking time at their sides.

Two by two, two by two, two by two . . .

And then, after nearly an hour, at the very end, drawn by the seventy-six—Lance had counted them—pair of oxen, came a small wooden cart with a group of men crowded close together standing up in it, one of them holding aloft a banner.

"State mil'try flag," Lance heard someone say.

He looked at the thirteen red and white stripes, the blue field with the single big white star and, inside the star, a coat-of-arms with a cow and a mountain and some pine trees. He was glad the State of Vermont had such a handsome flag.

The men in the cart were dressed to represent different trades. Some of them Lance recognized: Jake the Saddler with his awl, John Kilburn the Carpenter with compass and square, Cobbler Sam, waving his last.

Suddenly Lance knew he had had enough of the ox parade. Enough dried whortleberries and apple juice. Enough of the Fair.

He set off at a run toward the covered bridge.

Almost immediately he realized that everyone else was hurrying in precisely the same direction. Word of the log-hauling match had spread like a woods fire, and men, women, and children alike were bent on reaching the saw mill on Lower Creek as quickly as possible.

By the time Lance arrived, a circle of spectators three deep already ringed the clearing in front of the mill, and others were edging their way in. In the very center of the clearing, some ten rods from the log way, lay a great pine log to which two men, one of whom was Farmer Bob Evans, were hitching the little bay.

That must be Figure's owner! thought Lance, his heart beating fast with excitement. If he was right, and the man bending over the chain beside the farmer was really the music master from Randolph, why, that was the very person with whom, if the little stallion lost the match, he was determined to have an earnest talk.

Lance realized that a rough sort of fellow was squeezing into the circle at his elbow, and the next moment heard him burst into a guffaw of laughter. "So that's the critter folks been a-braggin' of!" He cupped a reddened hand over his mouth and spoke to Lance through a corner of it. " 'Twixt you and me, friend, I been here off 'n on all morning a-watching of 'em try ter git one hoss arter another ter pull that there log ten feet. Two on 'em weighed close ter twelve hunerd pound. Neither a one could budge it. They was twice that critter's size."

"You—you don't think he can do it?" asked Lance quickly, hopefully.

"Want ter lay a wager?" demanded the other eagerly.

Lance shook his head. "No," he said, "I don't want to lay any wager."

"Only a want-wit would!" retorted the other, and laughed his scornful laugh.

With the hitch adjusted to their evident satisfaction, both men straightened and stepped backward.

Farmer Evans lifted his hand, and instantly the crowd hushed until the only sound to be heard was the splashing of Lower Creek over the stones in its shallow bed.

"Neighbors," he said, "the little bay's owner and I have offered a gallon o' rum to any man whose horse will haul yonder pine log the ten rods to the mill in three pulls. So far, we've had plenty of takers, but nary a winner. Challenge still stands. Any here want to try?" He paused to look around him at the circle of faces.

There was no response.

"Neighbors," he went on, "we aim to better our own challenge. We claim this little stallion will haul that log he's hitched to the stiperlated distance o' ten rods in three pulls with any three men here present a-standing on it!"

A gasp rose from the spectators. Lance saw several of them glance at each other and shake their heads.

"I repeat, will any three men—"

A dozen men sprang forward.

"You!" said the farmer. "And you! And you!"

He chose the three who seemed the heaviest of those who had offered themselves, and they walked over to the log and balanced themselves upon it.

Lance hardly saw them. He had eyes only for the little bay, patiently waiting for the word to go. When it came, and Lance saw the shoulder muscles quiver under the silken smooth skin, the shapely feet lift, one by one, as the log with its burden moved slightly, and gradually more and more, while the crowd held its breath—then something unbelievable happened to Lance. He clenched his hands at his sides, and wished with all his heart and mind and soul that Figure would succeed.

A quarter of the way, a third, a half—

The little horse stopped, and heavily, like a single person, the crowd gave a long, deep sigh.

He started again, moving faster than he had moved before, and with less apparent effort. The men on the log wavered, recovered their balance.

Three quarters of the way—seven eighths—he was entitled to one more halt—he wasn't going to stop—he was—no. He reached the log-way swiftly, easily.

The crowd burst into cheer after cheer. Hats flew high in the air, and somebody shouted, "Hurrah for Bob Evans and the Randolph fiddler!"

Slowly Lance's clenched fists loosened, dropped to his sides, but his eyes were shining. He wished his father could have been with him to see what he had just seen. He wished . . . But whatever he was wishing he straightway forgot, as he was pushed forward with the surge of those who wanted to pat the little bay and shake hands with his owner and Farmer Evans.

The next thing he knew, he himself was close enough to the two men to hear what those who came up were saying, and suddenly he saw a gentleman in a beaver hat and long black frock coat put his hand on Figure's head and look about at the crowd, which was continually pressing closer.

"Friends," he said in a loud, clear voice, "you who have been fortunate enough to be here on this remarkable occasion will be proud to tell your children and your grandchildren that which you have witnessed. I even venture to prophesy this day will come to be held as a *great* day in the history of the State of Vermont, that it may even be commemorated as such. Therefore I suggest that this handsome, this marvellous creature be henceforth known, not by his present name of—what is his present name, sir? Figure? I thank you—Figure, but by the name of his proud and happy owner, Justin Morgan, who stands here by my side. Wherefore, I give you—*Justin Morgan!* May he father a noble line!"

The cold, sweet, wholesome tang of late afternoon in October filled Lance's nostrils as he walked back to the grist mill to find the Chapelles. He was like one who has just dreamed a vivid and lovely dream, and is not yet quite wakened from it. He was hardly aware that the sun was nearly set; that, however golden the tops of the mountains, their lower slopes were in shadow; that Fair Day had come and gone.

Mechanically he gave Cherry her supper of oats and stood beside her while she ate.

Waiting thus, he saw the Chapelles walking toward him. M'ma Chapelle, her arm through P'pa Chapelle's, looked tired but happy. The twins were plainly sleepy, very cross, and very, very sticky from a steady diet of peppermint sticks and apple juice. 'Tilda, her arms piled high with this and that, was chattering excitedly of all she had seen and done. "That man with the dancing bear—I won a three-legged race . . ."

"Tais-toi, Mathilde!" said P'pa Chapelle sharply. He spoke to Lance, and his face wore the expression it always did when he had something, or possibly two somethings, up his sleeve. "How ees eet now, mon fils? Ees eet that you weel go West weeth us?"

Lance didn't answer at once, and Pierre, a little impatiently, repeated his question. "Ees eet that you weel go West weeth us, Lance?"

Suddenly Lance seemed to find himself and to know what the answer to that question must be. He seemed to realize that all that had happened since he and his father had built the cabin on the little clearing had shaped his decision, and that nothing which had taken place this afternoon could change it.

He shook his head. "No," he said. "No, Mr. Chapelle. I'm staying in the State of Vermont."

'Tilda uttered a little shriek. "However will you get enough to eat?"

"I'll hire out for a job in the Iron Works at Bennington," said Lance. "I won't starve."

"He weel not starve," said Pierre, "and I don't theenk he weel get job in those Iron Works either. Tonight he weel come home weeth us. Tomorrow he weel pack all hees belongings, lak that old Eagle-eye, and weeth them he weel ride back here to Valley Mill. Ees that not so, Lance?"

Lance looked at him doubtfully. "I expect I'll be walking," he said.

Pierre shook his head. "No, I theenk not. I 'ave hoped you would go West, but I 'ave felt a—how you say eet?—hunch it weel not be so. But I 'ave one leetle more favor to ask. You 'ave already done the so great favor for M'ma and Mathilde and Jean and Jacques while their P'pa ees gone so long from home. But there ees one leetle, veree leetle favor more. Wash and Jeff I tak West. But Cherie—the leetle mare—no. I geev Cherie to you."

Lance's heart turned over. He could not possibly have heard what he thought he heard. He swallowed, but found it hard to speak. "You don't mean—?" he managed.

"But yes, mon ami. That I do mean. And she ees not truly a geeft. You 'ave earned her. I 'ave already told that Meester Justeen Morgan of Randolph how she ees not mine. He promised to be here—" Pierre broke off to stare about him, then gave a satisfied nod. "And he *ees* here!"

The next minute Lance found himself shaking hands with the Randolph fiddler.

"Mr. Chapelle tells me you are the owner of this little chestnut," he said pleasantly. "I noticed her early this morning. I have a plan in my head. Did you by any chance see my little Figure perform this afternoon?"

"Yes," said Lance, wondering what this was all about, "I did, sir."

"My friends tell me I'm a fool not to perpetuate a marvellous strain like that. Power, speed, beauty, tractability. How'd ye feel about going into the business of raising future Morgans along with me? Seems to me the country could use a line o' hosses inheriting the qualities of your little chestnut and my little bay. You don't have to decide now. Think it over. I'm spending the night with Bob Evans. If it strikes you as an attractive idea, meet me at his farm tomorrow." He turned to go.

Before he had taken two steps, Lance grabbed his arm. "Do I have to think it over, Mr. Morgan? Do I *have* to? I know my answer right now. I'd rather do what you asked me than—than be the owner of the whole of the Bennington Iron Works!"

A moment later, Lance found himself alone with Cherry. Mr. Morgan was on his way to find Farmer Evans. P'pa Chapelle was herding his little family toward the ox cart. Over in the meadow, Fair-weary men and women, some with candle-lighted lanterns, were emptying the booths and taking down the signs and bunting.

The soft wind of twilight had come down from the mountains, and was rustling the crisp leaves of the sugar maples. The sweet-sharp smell of balsam drifted in from the nearby forest. What was it that song of Tin Peddler Joe had said about this land? "The best that e'er was seen for soil and air."

Cherry, throwing up her head, gave an impatient whinny. Lance reached for the bridle, sprang into the saddle, and the two of them were on their way.

END